A SHALLOW
SHIFTING
PRECIPICE

A SHALLOW SHIFTING PRECIPICE

STEPHEN COLINCO

TATE PUBLISHING
AND ENTERPRISES, LLC

Published by Tate Publishing & Enterprises, LLC
127 E. Trade Center Terrace | Mustang, Oklahoma 73064 USA
1.888.361.9473 | www.tatepublishing.com

Tate Publishing is committed to excellence in the publishing industry. The company reflects the philosophy established by the founders, based on Psalm 68:11,
"The Lord gave the word and great was the company of those who published it."

Book design copyright © 2016 by Tate Publishing, LLC. All rights reserved.
Cover design by Bill Francis Peralta
Interior design by Richell Balansag

Published in the United States of America

ISBN: 978-1-68254-856-1
1. Fiction / Christian / General
2. Fiction / War & Military
16.04.14

For Pang, the most interesting man I know.

Definitions

ABU: Army Battle Uniform

HCLOS: High Capacity Line-Of-Sight Radio.

FAST Helmet: A lightweight combat ballistic helmet worn by Special Forces operators.

HUMVEE: High Mobility Multipurpose Wheeled Vehicle (HMMWV) used by US and

NATO military personnel.

LZ: Landing Zone.

MRAP: Mine Resistant Ambush Protected vehicle

NATO: North Atlantic Treaty Organization.

Prologue

In the summer of 2008, US forces recently encountered indirect mortar and direct small arms fire from Taliban and Al-Qaeda fighters entrenched in the mountain ranges of Hindu Kush. The 503rd Infantry Regiment, embedded with the 173rd Airborne Division, force capacity of 150 light and armored infantry, is garrisoned outside the village of Wanat. Captain Marlon Coe, commanding officer of 2nd battalion, 3rd Special Operations group, was ordered to the village of Wanat.

Chapter One

Afghanistan is a paradox. Alexander the Great calls it, "The land of kings that could not be conquered." It is a sandbox of modernized European civilizations colliding with ancient western Asia. Its tumultuous history embroiled in violence passed on through generations of warring tribes had long existed before the birth of Christ. Its cultural, religious, and political dichotomy is fragile, delicately fused by segmented populations comprised of bold tribal lines steeped in centuries-old tradition that transcends through modern age. The vast, unsolicited lands weaving through its imposing mountainous regions are nature's marvels; a formidable backbone that cannot be subdued. Neither its middle-eastern neighbors nor its European counterparts could subdue the entire country. It is a country mired under draconian principles. The power vacuum inherited from the demise of Soviet occupation opened the door to the rise of the heavy-handed rule of the Taliban—a ruling party who imposed stringent, liturgical Islamic Shari'a law for decades. Now, it represents as the crucible of American military might and political resolve.

05:30, 14ᵗʰ July 2008. Nuristan Province, mountain village of Wanat, between Pakistan and Afghanistan border.

The weather was a bit frosty, and the nippy air lingered on from the midnight hour. The copious lunar reflection unveiled a luminous sky that crept over the valley broke the arid fog; its soft permeation illuminated the base. Everything lay silent. And with quiet declaration, a crescendo of brilliant light ascended from the east, piercing through the opaque night; its rays sifting the morning dew, wilting the shadows over the horizon, and revealing the vast steep rice patties of the Hindu Kush. Its radiance ushered in the warmth of day, reaping the stubborn cold. The inevitable countdown to zero hour was near, culminating a new dawn of uncertainty. Inside the base, the atmosphere remained quiet but tense; its silence was drowned out by the dry gust of wind and fine desert sand seeping through the crevices of the plywood doors.

He was wide awake, unable to retain much rest from the previous day assessing the whole battle scenario for the upcoming mission. The rugged six-by-ten sleeping quarter surrounded by one-inch thick plywood was evenly partitioned within a metallic warehouse. Each room, crudely assembled, formed a sandlot designed to house a battalion of soldiers, administrative staff, and private contractors. Inside the room, a small three-inch thick mattress sunk over the rusted metal bed nestled on the far left corner. An unstained makeshift wooden desk leaning against the plywood wall occupied half of the space. Every section of the wall was filled with a hodgepodge of family pictures, military photos, maps, and magazine cutouts. His ABU, wrinkled and dusty, hung loosely on the makeshift closet door adjacent to his bedpost. A small fluorescent light dangling above the shallow ceiling barely illuminated the room, revealing a morose atmosphere; only the flickering screen of his laptop appeared lively. His ammo gear hung on a five-inch hook nailed against the door, his rucksack rested against the table, and his M-4 carbine hung squarely over his head, ready to be used within a moment's notice. There was a musty scent that lingered inside the room; a distinct odor from old brewed coffee grounds, worn socks, and sweat-stained clothes that lingered on for days not far removed from a college dorm room. He had grown privy to the seclusion for the past twelve months, accustomed to the daily grind. He had anticipated conducting far fewer routine patrols than any usual days. The excitement and angst during the initial part of his deployment has now grown senile and customary; nothing out of the ordinary seemed to rev his excitement. He had hoped for this day to come; a reprieve from the monotonous days far stretched in between that felt tepid and dull. Countless days had passed since he had experienced the glory of combat. And it was time to reinvigorate the senses; the lure and intense rush of adrenaline was addictive. A great battle was ticking near.

For Marlon, this mission would conclude his fifth and last tour of duty. Although the desire for combat surged fast in his veins, he is being pulled away from the field and relegated into a desk job reserved for senior officers. He was being groomed to take command of the brigade, which required him to command away from the front lines. His military career was steering toward a mundane civilian life, perhaps to devote his time on fatherhood; a place where men of action were destined to fade.

After fifteen years of service, serving with his men on the field, he was tasked to lead a clandestine operation and take the fight to the enemy; this may be his last hurrah before hanging his combat gear. The planning and impending battle built up for the past two days has finally reached the precipice. He was the architect of the mission, and he relished the moment with his men intensely, far exceeding the joys of a quaint family life. For him, this anticipated promotion was finally coming to fruition. Deep down, he resented the idea of relinquishing his post to operate in the field alongside his men, but age had caught up to him, impugning his physical capacity to lead and operate at an optimal level. The impending battle would be his glorious exit, and he was priming to unveil his magnum opus.

As he prepped his weapons, a hard knock came at the exact time. "Captain Coe," Sergeant Miller hollered outside the door. "First Sergeant Miller," Marlon replied. "Are the men ready?" He promptly asked. "The men are ready, sir!" Miller asserted. "Good, I'll be right out!" Marlon said as he buckled his sidearm. After placing on his combat vest, one of his men knocked on the plywood door. Few seconds passed and another knock came through. "Sir, Specialist Yratta. Permission to enter?" Yratta blurted. "Come in, Yratta!" he replied. Yratta entered the room and handed him a small manila envelope, its creases were slightly worn; its white color turned beige as evidence age. Marlon took the envelope. It was a letter from Georgia, a thin piece of letter from his wife. He grinned. "Thanks," he said as he examined the letter. It has been weeks since he had received a small piece of envelope in contrast to larges packages that previously arrived. "Is there anything I can get you, sir?" Yratta asked. "No, you're good, Specialist. Wait for me outside and get ready to roll out."

"Sir!" Yratta firmly replied. He stood erect and stepped out in a casual manner.

That morning, Marlon was tasked to lead a small contingent unit to capture or kill a high-value target; a high ranking officer who was responsible for the recent spate of attacks against NATO soldiers garrisoned near Wanat. Soft Intel indicated that he was hiding inside the village. Marlon's primary mission was to capture or kill the target. His secondary mission was to ascertain the status of the local residents and regain the confidence of the village elders. His team is comprised of six green berets from the 547th embedded with a squad of newly trained Afghani soldiers tasked to establish a base inside the village; these soldiers signified the emerging standard military of the country. Both teams were escorted by a squad of twelve infantry soldiers from the 503rd Infantry Brigade; their main task is to secure the perimeter inside the village and reinforce the operators when necessary.

The men were prepped and ready, gearing up quietly, patiently waiting for their commanding officer to appear. Their battalion commander briefed the team specifically tasked for a critical operation eight hours prior to their mission. Due to the plan's clandestine nature, coupled with the element of surprise and the complexity of the terrain, Marlon opted to take the team on the ground instead of a quick airborne insertion, utilizing armor over maneuverability.

There were twenty-four men tasked for the operation: four teams comprised of six men were assigned to a squad. The six green berets were handpicked by Marlon (all were over the age of thirty). These men are highly trained for a specific role, well equipped with state-of-the-art weapon systems-they wore distinct FAST helmet, and advanced body armor. They epitomize the modern-day Spartans-an elite fighting unit comprised of professional sanctioned killers. These unconventional fighters of reputable combat prowess earned the fear and loathing of the Taliban; they are finesse operators and experts in any method of violence. Each man sported a beard and wore dark-rimmed Oakley sunglasses that guise the eyes of bottled aggression. Their steely gaze exudes an aura of invincibility; an innate sense of haughtiness reserved for the select few. And their vacant eyes reveal a hollow but empathic virtue desensitized by human frailty stemming from their inevitable descent into the abyss of human depravity; an acquired pragmatism and the penultimate result of nihilistic transcendence for the calloused bastards of war.

They are a tight-knit fraternity, a brotherhood of men bonded by blood and baptized in deadly firefights; a coterie of characters soaked in caustic bravado. Each man was in peak physical condition evident by the heavy weight they hauled conducting routine patrols; they carried at least forty to sixty pounds of gear, ammunition, and weaponry.

The majority had years of combat experience plainly etched on the surface of their skin and blended in contrasting colors. And each man earned a distinction *De Oppresso Liber* in black ink meticulously crafted on their chest. The team was comprised of seasoned veterans who served in several tours in Iraq and Afghanistan. All are accustomed to the art of war and well versed in *Pashto*. They are molded for specific roles: train the local militia sanctioned by the state, gather Intel on the ground, and if necessary, capture or kill any suspected enemy combatants.

Marlon, as his usual routine, said a brief silent prayer. He zipped up his vest and ran his hands through his ammunition belt and walked briskly towards the three desert-clad Humvee's and two MRAPs parked in a single file; its engines grumbled on the cracked dirt.

Everyone on his team noticed the Afghani's apprehension to conduct the mission. His six-man team was itching for a fight, but the rest appeared timid—perhaps it was due to the ubiquitous purpose of the mission and their lack of combat experience. While the operators were eager for combat they appeared calm but eager—this was the profession they volunteered, and their lax demeanor revealed a strong resolve to execute orders and accomplish the mission. The whole team was quite aware of the day's unpredictable outcome, and they were cautious, bent on finishing the task without incurring further casualties or complications throughout the duration. And each member was counting down to the end of their tour—most were adamant for redeployment. But they were resolute, fiercely loyal and champions to their cause. And Marlon Coe was a leader they blindly followed.

Marlon is a competent, seasoned officer. He is instinctive and brash. He earned his rank as a career military soldier in the army right after high school in 1994 having served two tours in Iraq with the 173rd Airborne Division. Two years later, he joined the Airborne Rangers as a non-commissioned officer in the 2nd Ranger Battalion, 75th Regiment. He enrolled in a college program as a part-time student during his tenure as a non-commissioned officer in the Army. In 2002, he graduated with a bachelor's degree in classical history, barely making it through being ranked near the bottom of his class. After Iraq, he entered and graduated from Officer Candidate School and Infantry Officer Basic Course then joined the Green Berets soon after. And after fifteen years of grunt work, he was handpicked by senior staff and groomed to command the battalion. A career in the military was a promising venue, an occupation where he felt a sense of purpose and direction. Standing alongside his men in the battlefield satiated his urge for battlefield glory-like a boy craving adventure. For him, nothing else seemed to matter outside of the military life.

Marlon Coe was born in 1975 to Elijah Coe and Caroline Beam. Growing up in Dixie in an African American family had a significant impact in his upbringing. Marlon, a soft-spoken man, was a great-grandson of a former slave. Elijah and Caroline married in their late teens, but the couple was unable to conceive a child; they were resigned to the reality that she was barren, but a miraculous event led to the birth of their firstborn son. Caroline was thirty-five when Charles was born.

Marlon's father was a laborer and his mother was a housekeeper. Elijah and Caroline bore a second child two years later. Marlon was born on an unusually cold day in late July 1975. Charles, the older of the two, serves as a Southern Baptist minister in Austin, Texas. The two brothers were inseparable during their adolescent years, but drifted since Marlon joined the military.

Caroline Marlon died of brain tumor during Marlon's second tour in Iraq. The death devastated his father and isolated the two siblings. Caroline was the glue that kept the family intact, and she was the one who kept her husband grounded. She was Marlon's confidant and spiritual mentor, and she influenced Charles to attend seminary and become a minister. Despite her soft-spoken demeanor, she was a stern disciplinarian who rectified the boys' onerous behavior with a switch, and it kept the boy's out of trouble throughout their adolescence. Due to lack of available education and poverty, she regularly brought the boys to the library to fill their voracious appetite for reading, equipping them with the knowledge and education they solely lacked. Charles was fascinated with literature and science where he excelled, while Marlon immersed himself with poetry and history, soaking every book on military exploits and heroes of the past.

Caroline's death convinced Marlon to remain in the service where he found solace alongside his men. For him, there was a sense of urgency and substance in the middle of a firefight. For fifteen years, he rose through the ranks as an infantry enlistee, then later as a junior officer. His subordinates admired his leadership, and his superiors were impressed with his combat experience and brilliant tactical awareness.

Marlon grew up as a scrawny kid. His timid, insecure, but stubborn disposition did not bode well under two strict disciplinarians. His upbringing was fraught with physical and emotional strain under the ire of his short-tempered, alcoholic father.

As Marlon approached the men, he looked at his first sergeant standing alongside the men. "Sergeant Miller, let's hear that beautiful prayer of yours," he blurted.

"Sir!" the Sergeant replied. Miller gently bowed his head. "But you, O Lord, are a shield around me, my glory, and the one who lifts my head high. I call out to the Lord, and he answers me from his holy mountain. I lie down and sleep, I wake again, because the Lord sustains me. I will not fear though tens of thousands assail me on every side. Arise, Lord! Deliver me, my God! Strike all my enemies on the jaw; break the teeth of the wicked." Then Miller opened his eyes and looked at the men, "From the Lord comes deliverance. May your blessing be on my Green Berets!"

"Whoa!" All the men chanted.

Then Marlon and his team mounted the trucks.

That day, they proceeded to execute their mission at the village where the locals and the military converged.

"Echo Two-Four Alpha, this is Whiskey Five-Six, over! Echo Two-Four Alpha, this is Whiskey Five-Six, over!" he called on the radio to the command center to check the clarity of his radio link.

"Whiskey Five-Six, this is Echo Two-Four Alpha-Read you loud and clear," the man responded.

"Echo Two-Four, we're heading down range, permission to execute," Marlon asserted.

"Roger that! Execute mission, Captain. Good luck!" his commanding officer replied.

Marlon made a subtle glance to the driver as the whole column rolled out of their fortified garrison, weaving its way through a maze of four-foot concrete barricades. All five vehicles packed with men and materials began their mission at dawn. Daylight impetuously crept down behind them from the east over the mountain ridge. Their mirage grew over the rising heat as their apparitions shrunk, revealing billows of dust clouds in their wake.

As they went further, angst and trepidation grew stronger of the unknown; each man wore their game face, their quiet façade cloaked their racing thoughts; everyone was edgy. Time seemingly slowed down as the vehicles rushed over the packed dirt, rolling fast and hard.

Each vehicle was at least fifty to sixty feet apart. Marlon, sitting at the front passenger seat of the third vehicle, radioed the first vehicle to take a different route to the village six miles away. The roads were typically booby-trapped with crudely made improvised explosive devices hidden beneath the unpaved, rugged road. Driving through the rugged terrain on the side of the road fared better of eluding any ambush by the enemy hidden above the mountain ridge and who could easily spot the convoy approaching from miles away.

Marlon surveyed the map to examine the open areas vulnerable to incoming fire. The steep ridge to his left offered little comfort for safety— giving the enemy a clear vantage point. Intel from the previous night concluded that unknown numbers of Taliban fighters sneaked in under the cover of darkness prepping to engage them. Informants hinted that the enemy dug ditches and rerouted the small water stream to disguise their movement. It was estimated that two to four hundred Taliban and Al-Qaeda fighters banded together for the initial assault against the US garrison stationed outside of the village. The local residents gave little hint of the enemy's whereabouts, fearing brutal reprisals from the Taliban. Marlon was fully aware of the impending assault. Their presence placed the residents in such precarious predicament against the Taliban.

After they left the base, the radio crackled from the front vehicle, "Ahh-tention ladies and gentlemen. This is your captain speaking. On behalf of the crew, I want to welcome you to the finest American transportation system, Air Jordans." Miller announced. Upon hearing this, the men laughed.

"My name is Captain Bin-Laden…and I am pleased to announce that we will be serving peanuts on this trip. I myself will personally serve you peanuts on a platter doused with Afghan chocolate and cream. It is imported…from Afghanistan. Mmm, good! Now, just to let you know, this trip also comes with a free tour. Take a look at your right, and you will see the beautiful sandy plains—all crowded with booby traps, poppy fields, and scorpions. It goes on…and on…and on, well, until you reach the desert. And to your left are mountains…lots and lots of it; perfect for snow, ice-capades, and mountain biking, or couples hiking.

"Now, folks, I must admit. It is a tad dangerous…so make sure that you pack lots of warm blankets and sandals. You'll never know when you will need it to greet our friends, the Taliban. Well, I'm excited to announce that we will be guests of honor to our neighbors in the village, so bring lots of booze. Oh, and um…make sure to bring your appetite… and the metal detector. You'll never know when you will need it for treasure hunting.

"And finally, make sure you have clean shorts. I hope you brought a new pair of underwear-because where we're going, folks…well…its Willie Wonk's IED factory full of rocks and nails. In a short while, I will be taking off the No Smoking sign and the Seatbelt sign off. You are not, I repeat, you are not free to move about the cabin since there's no space to move. So, please keep your hands to yourself and have a coke and a smile.

"Oh, and one last thing, the trip may take a shortcut…somewhere. So, make sure you do not ask for beverages, or I swear I will stop this car. So, on behalf of Air…Jordans and Uncle Sam, we would like to extend our thanks."

Marlon picked up the radio, "Good one, First Sergeant. Don't forget to serve my peanuts on the way." He smiled.

"Roger, roger."

The rest of the men laughed hysterically, lightening the mood of the team and easing the tense atmosphere.

Chapter Two

They arrived at the outskirts of the village at daybreak. Marlon envisioned every potential scenario and summed up the details of unpredictable events that could unravel at any moment. He's aware of the enemy's presence but uncertain of the extent of their capacity. Hazardous moments lay ahead upon entrance and exit. He and his men were exposed to the typical combat encounters, desensitized by threats from constant enemy fire. The Green Berets appeared cool, but the rest of the men were edgy.

As they forged ahead, they came across a very tall man who suddenly appeared at the middle of the road. He stood erect at the far distance, over a heap of packed dirt, holding a burro at the bit. He was undaunted, staring intently at the fast incoming convoy. The men in the front vehicle were caught off guard to see him appear out of nowhere.

The radio crackled. "Sir, one potential combatant closing in."

"Copy that!" Marlon answered, thinking of worst case scenario while trying to ascertain the safest approach. He paused and replied on the radio. "Stand by!" he blurted. "Ready weapons and ammo!"

The men immediately cocked their rifles; their faces turned gritty. The machine gunner on the middle turret turned towards the man, cocked then aimed the squad automatic weapon mounted on the roof.

"Jake, get Snoop ready," he ordered the dog handler over the radio. The dog handler rode on the second vehicle waiting to disembark. Marlon pondered briefly. "*If I stop, we could get caught in the middle of an ambush. If I don't, that man may be carrying explosives. This is not good! Not good!*" He sighed. "*Typical! We need to keep moving.*" He picked up the radio, "Jake, how long is this going to take?"

"Two minutes tops!" Jake replied.

"Okay, listen carefully. Get snoop out to check out the man. Signal once it's clear!"

"Roger that!"

Marlon ordered the team over the radio, "Order the front to stop—standby."

The convoy halted to inspect the man who stood at the road motionless, facing the mountain cliffs. Then his head turned straight at the approaching vehicle. He appeared fearless; his face showed no sign or hint of threat, and his posture was lax, absent of any belligerent motive.

As ordered, Jake Wychyck quickly disembarked and took the trained Belgian Malinois by the harness and proceeded to inspect the man standing still. The dog cocked his head and refused to move. Snoop sheepishly sat down and whimpered, without barking or panting.

"What's wrong, buddy? Jake asked, surprised to see the dog's timid behavior. He's never witnessed the animal behave in such a tamed manner. "Let's go, Snoop! C'mon, boy! Here we go!" Jake prodded. Snoop, so accustomed to bomb search, so eager to follow his handler's lead, refused to stand and move further. He simply sat on the gravel, without fussing, refusing to heed his master's call.

Marlon impatiently yelled out, "Jake! What's going on?"

"He's not moving sir!"

"Not moving? He's a dog!" he cried out.

"Sorry, sir, I've never seen this myself."

"Great!" he thought to himself. *"The man is standing there, unmoved, and the dog just stares at him as if he knows him. Snoop's afraid, and I've never seen him this scared."*

"Jake, the dog's name is Snoop for Pete's sake. What's the point of that name if he can't sniff?" Marlon blurted over the radio.

"Sir?" Jake replied. "Umm, don't know what to tell you... He's spooked!" The dog was specifically trained to sniff any hint of explosives from a good distance. He'd been a part of the team since they arrived in Afghanistan. For Marlon, to see the animal behave erratically, whimpering at the sight of a stranger seemed out of place. Something was amiss, and Jake was dumbfounded. Typically, the insurgents would plant the improvised explosive device and leave. Sometimes they will observe the enemy behind some cover far from the blast zone.

21

Marlon realized that they could not afford to waste more time, he needed to act decisively.

Tapping the side of the door, he looked at Jake. "Okay, mount up!" he yelled at the men on the radio over his left shoulder.

Jake appeared embarrassed of Snoop's vehemence. Nevertheless, Jake was relieved to forego the awkward situation and seeing his dog's action was highly unusual, something that he's never seen or heard throughout his deployment. As the convoy began to move slowly, Marlon ordered the front vehicle to observe the man's actions. He grabbed the radio and ordered his team, "Anything suspicious, anything at all…If he sneezes, take him down!"

"Roger that!" the men replied.

"Slow down, but don't go too slow under ten," he ordered.

The first vehicle cautiously slowed down when the column approached closer; each man carefully observed the man standing idly by, waiting for them to pass, but his eyes remained fixated on Marlon.

Marlon peaked through the side of his window with a pair of compact binoculars. He was worried and prickly, and his face grew flustered as they drew closer. The man was at close proximity for any potential attack. Marlon's thoughts raised; his eyes were locked at the man-time froze. He squinted through his binoculars and couldn't make up the man's outfit. He appeared taller than a typical Afghan. He stood unfazed, possessing an aura of invincibility. The power of his presence was unrestrained; his countenance was sublime. A white turban was wrapped his head, and his clothes were tattered and worn, but his beard was full and white; they were as white as snow. He appeared seasoned and long in years, but his face was unblemished and fair, absent of any wrinkles and pernicious intent. What stood out to Marlon were his eyes; they reflected the glaring color of day, piercing but gentle. Marlon felt his presence-like a wave of storm rolled beneath a lush garden, calm but powerful. Marlon thought to himself, "*This guy's not going to move. If we fire warning shots, the enemy will know we're here. If we honk our horns, they will know we're close.*" He lifted the radio right on his lips. "Go around him!" he blurted.

"Sir?" The man on the other end asked, slightly confused.

"Go around him, Sergeant." he calmly said.

"Roger that! Moving around haji," the driver replied.

The first vehicle passed him from the left near the river stream to avoid the steep mountain cliff to his right which seemed more ideal for Marlon to navigate and avoid any present danger. In case of an attack, the driver would not be endangered, and the column doesn't get bogged by the riverbed or the large boulders.

The man stood where the foot of the mountain ridge converged on the edge of the largest river gap, a narrow pass where an ambush was an ideal position to inflict optimum casualty. The road spanned about ten meters wide. The steep rocky mountain and the large boulders strewn along the pass gave the enemy a significant vantage point for ambush. The Taliban, hidden under cover, could easily mount an effective attack against them with minimal effort and little impunity.

Marlon was a bit annoyed by this unwelcomed predicament, but he had no choice. The man and his burro would not budge, and they could not linger and wait for the man to move. Everyone remained quiet as they approached him. They noticed the radio crackling, then it went silent as they reached a bottleneck. The moment turned peaceful and quiet, until they passed him. One by one, the vehicle carefully passed the tall stranger. As Marlon glanced at the man, he noticed his eyes were emerald green and clear as crystal. He had never seen someone with such fair skin and piercing eyes. The man looked straight at him, implying something amiss—he felt his heart trembling in fear. As he passed, the man kept his eyes on him. Although he was curious as to what just transpired, Marlon simply brushed it off. "*Weird*!" he thought, "Always something new!" he whispered.

"What's that, sir?" his driver asked candidly.

"Nothing…nothing at all," he mumbled, shrugging his shoulders. "Is this common here in your country, Khaled?" Marlon asked his translator sitting at the right passenger seat.

The translator couldn't find any fitting reply for the unexplained event; he shook his head in disbelief and smiled.

"See, this is common in the States. Right, private?"

"Whoa!" The driver chuckled.

"You know what?' Marlon asked, 'You know what this place could use?"

"No, sir, what would that be?" Khaled replied.

"Grass. Lots and lots of it.' he scoffed. 'There's no freakin' grass around, just shrubs. You won't make it here...as a landscaper," he said as the men chuckled.

They stopped a quarter of a mile outside of the village. The six berets quickly disembarked and approached the village on foot, quietly pacing through ripe poppy fields. This gave them an upper hand and the element of surprise. They carefully navigated through the fields in a single file, tracing their footsteps to avoid any planted improvised explosive devices; each man walked ten to fifteen meters apart.

Sergeant Miller led the team as point-man, handling a metal detector several meters ahead of them. Jake and Snoop followed suit sniffing for any potential combatants. They walked stealthily through the entrance and up the narrow pass.

Each team member was assigned a specific task; two squads were assigned to secure the perimeter outside the village while Marlon and his team conducted house-to-house searches. The remaining teams from the 503ʳᵈ were placed on standby to man the mortar emplacements.

As they arrived at the main road an old man meandering on the sidewalk immediately spotted them, then he hastened to the house nearby. Within minutes, the rest of the men immediately ran towards one of the soldiers with utmost disregard for safety.

Marlon and his team grew suspicious as clamoring arose amongst the inhabitants. One of the village elders approached Miller. Thinking that he may be wired with explosives, Miller instinctively tackled the man to the ground without any hesitation, but the man was unarmed-causing further suspicions with the locals. The man stood up, groaning in pain, uttering words that made Khaled blush. He informed the translator that the Taliban had abandoned the village that previous night, sneaking out of the village under the cover of darkness along with several hostages. The Taliban beheaded the village elder upon their departure to incite fear. During this time, the fleeing enemy scouts spotted Marlon and his team as they fled to the mountains.

After several minutes of random searches, they found no signs of enemy presence within the vicinity. Marlon ordered the rest of his team to regroup and set up a perimeter. Much to his chagrin, he must now undertake a new mission: secure the village and bolster the partnership—a public relations nightmare he sees with disdain.

He radioed the team, ordering them to secure the perimeter around the village. The convoy passed the first obstacle one by one, and they sped up to the village a bit tardy from their anticipated arrival. The column eased and stopped at the middle of the village; each one angled to the side to avert any casualties in cases of any abrupt incoming enemy fire. Once they found the safest area, they immediately disembarked while a gunner stood fast on each vehicle gun turret. The mud walls were riddled with pockmarks from previous combat engagements, a vivid reminder of the Taliban's brutal retribution. They sensed an impending firefight unraveling due to Marlon's arrival. Nevertheless, they welcomed them with strong apprehension—they simply had no choice.

"Sergeant Framm!" Marlon hollered to his platoon sergeant, "Set me a defensive perimeter."

"Sir!" the man replied instantly.

"Sergeant Miller, let's go ahead and say hi to our neighbors…shall we?" he noted in jest.

"Think our neighbors got any extra sugar I could borrow?" Miller asked facetiously.

Marlon grinned, "That, or an AK,'" he replied, loosening his helmet, "'Game face on."

"Roger," Miller calmly replied.

They came and spoke with the village elders along with their Afghani translator. The village elders were adamant to welcome the uninvited guests; they appeared anxious to see the Americans. The atmosphere grew tense in a short period. The elders were obstinate, growing annoyed every minute Marlon and his men lingered. Their eyes were deep and desperate, and their demeanor displayed heightened trepidation as Marlon and his cohorts continued their discourse, hoping to encourage and extract valuable information about the enemy's whereabouts.

The men sat along on the dirt floor of the house, sharing tea and bread as customary, each one representing his family. The elders wore long thick lungee while the young men sported traditional topi coupled with rugged bright salwar kameez under their dingy chapan coats, intertwined with their baggy trousers and oversized vests (the colorful chapan coats signified their high economic status). These men were land owners who farmed opium and wheat. They are highly religious and liturgical, and they held on to strict traditional practices passed on for generations. They welcomed their guests with utmost generosity but feared the Taliban's violent reprisal for abetting the enemy. Their loyalty lay solely on tribal lines, and they were easily swayed by monetary bribe or by the victorious side, which could cause a dynamic shift and influence the outcome of the battle. Marlon and his men were fully aware of this cultural fore, and it made their mission more unpredictable, fraught with fatal outcomes. The mission was simple, but the event could turn for the worse at any moment. He and his men were out in the open at the center of a volatile situation, and they must remain at high alert while projecting a cool demeanor to ease the tension and crystallize the fragile trust between them and the locals.

"As-sala'am alaikum," Marlon greeted the leader, tapping his chest with his right hand.

Pressing on his chest, the elder replied, "Alaikum as-sala'am."

Marlon turned to his translator. "Tell him…tell him that we are here to offer gratitude and assistance."

The man obliged and spoke local dialect.

The Pashto held strong ties with the Taliban since the Taliban's rise to power, having fought alongside the Mujahidin and the Taliban during the Russo-Afghan war. The Pashto culture is steeped in tradition strongly held for generations. Nuristan province remains as one of the poorest provinces in Afghanistan, and it is a hotbed for insurgents who undermine NATO's rebuilding efforts brazenly disrupting civil progress with deadly, indiscriminate killing. Nuristan is located on the mountainous regions bordering Afghanistan and Pakistan. This area is ideal for many Pakistani Taliban fighters, who freely cross into Afghanistan with little impunity. It is a hotbed of intense skirmishes between the US against Al-Qaeda and their Taliban counterparts.

Marlon stared intently at the man's eyes, "Tell him if there's anything that we can do to offer assistance."

The translator continued his polite discourse with the elder as he invited them in for tea. The elder accommodated the captain and his first sergeant and entered a small house and joined the meeting with a few village leaders. They sat on the dirt floor and began a dialogue to ascertain the current situation and determine a common ground to assist and improve the economic plight of the whole village. The elders were growing petulant, adamant to divulge any information pertaining to the foreign fighters across the border, and it was deemed reprehensible to accommodate the Americans and turn against the Taliban. The elders, along with their families, face swift retribution from the Taliban for any evidence of fraternizing and cooperation with the Americans. As Marlon expected, the discourse remained soft and shallow.

Marlon was increasingly flustered as the meeting dragged on, hoping to extract valuable intel on the enemy's whereabouts, weaponry, and force capacity, only to be undermined by meaningless chatter.

The meeting went over half an hour when his radioman relayed a message from central command. Marlon excused himself while his first sergeant remained along with the translator to continue the dialogue between the village elders.

As he exited the building, he noticed a boy, merely in his teens, entering the house. He wore a long white shirt, several sizes larger, disguising his bony frame. Marlon felt the innocence in him when he looked directly at him and saw the sparkle in his eyes-charming but anxious. There was no hint of ill motive, but rather a heightened sense of fear. Marlon smiled at him, but the boy reciprocated with a sheepish glance. Marlon tapped him gently over his white topi sitting flatly over his thick, shaggy hair, but the boy never flinched, looking down as he passed through the doorway.

The Afghanis guarding the entrance saw the boy and smiled at him, barely frisking him for any weapons hidden beneath his clothing in fear of stoking any offenses or inappropriate conduct at the sight of the residents, and the lingering morning heat and the heavy combat gear had began to take its toll on each man. His mother stood nearby, prodding the boy to enter, insisting that the boy needed to see his father.

Marlon looked back and proceeded to take the call from his radioman standing by the nearest Humvee parked at least twenty meters from the house.

"Sir, Colonel Moreo!" the radioman firmly said as he handed the phone to his commanding officer.

"This is Whiskey Five-Six," he answered.

"Cap, we received intel that fighters are moving towards your vicinity. E-T-A thirty mikes," the man on the radio warned.

"Force capacity?" he asked with urgency.

"Approximately fifty to two hundred," the man replied. "Light to heavily armed."

Marlon's eyes narrowed. "Roger that. Any reinforcements?"

"Negative, no bird inbound for another thirty. I repeat, no bird inbound for another thirty mikes," Moreo replied. "Choppers are grounded due to weather-until we receive a green light from command. Artillery support is on standby for active contact, over."

The warning did not bode well, there was no time to make a hasty retreat where the inevitable collision between them standing against a larger force was brewing. His eyes zinged from every angle, his mind raising as he braced for an impending blood-bath. *"Geez, Twenty-four men against two hundred in a hostile territory? No helos in sight. Better ready the men and brace for contact,"* he thought. He gathered himself, "Get the first sergeant out here!" he yelled out to one of the men standing by.

The man nodded and immediately fetched Sergeant Miller and Khaled who was still inside the house. Marlon followed suit and proceeded to return to the house. Without warning a bomb detonated inside the meeting place. The powerful blast hurled Marlon and his radioman standing outside of the house into the hood of the first humvee parked ten meters away.

The sudden impact shocked the men and immediately brought panic to the whole village. Marlon's ears were ringing. He was slow to recover as he lifted himself on the front grill of the first vehicle. His radioman was unconscious and unresponsive. He slowly crawled over to him and yelled at him to get up. He leaned over and shook him violently hoping to awaken him, but it was futile. After checking his neck for pulse, he realized that Robben was dead. The blast hurled him to the side of the vehicle head-on and broke his neck, killing him instantly. Marlon gathered himself and stood up while the men instinctively hunkered down and immediately took defensive positions in and around the convoy behind the cover of their vehicles. Marlon turned and looked up, then his eyes widened- the house was no longer there. The place was obliterated from the force of the explosion.

Specialist Kevin Spate grabbed him by the arm screeaming, "Cap! Cap!" Marlon was still dazed and disoriented. "Captain Coe! Your orders, sir!"

Marlon could barely hear the man screaming at him, all he heard were the drowning screams and gunshots popping. He could only read his lips to decipher every word and the jumbled sounds. The ringing lingered on for almost a minute as he slowly came to his senses.

Chapter Three

The digital alarm clock sitting at the wooden table blared off at 5:30 a.m. as usual. Daylight was fast approaching. Marlon, unable to escape the lurid dreams, kept staring at the popcorn-white ceiling-his eyes open and his eyelids heavy. He tried haplessly but couldn't gain any lengthy meaningful sleep throughout the night. These prolonged doldrums grew longer for countless nights; he'd dozed off, only to be shaken up by flashes of firefights, his body soaked in cold sweat.

Eight months had passed since the events at Wanat. Marlon was alone, lying in bed, wearing only his brown army-issued boxer briefs covered by a thin white sheet over his waist. The vivid memories of combat raced through his mind every pallid morning, recalling the gory battles etched deeply in his psyche. The partial loss of his hearing, the smell of burning sulfur, and a cacophony of cannons exploding, guns popping, and screams of dying civilians corroded his sanity; sleep eventually became his adversary. But it was Framm's heinous act that haunted him. The tragic loss of innocent lives from the past drove him to the edge.

The present offered little hope of closure. He was brooding, and his demeanor revealed a hint melancholy. He had succumbed to another lull and tried to swallow a .45-caliber hallow-point bullet the previous night, only to freeze at the last moment from pulling the trigger. As much as the pain was inflamed, he never came through with it; he was needed for the next few days for inexplicable reasons and the inevitable military tribunal was critical to exonerate him from the tragic events at Wanat. For him, his magnum opus turned disastrous. It brought him to the nadir of his military career. Hope, although faded, loomed close, as he longed for redemption to absolve past mistakes. And the thought of his daughter gave him a slight semblance of humanity.

The clock blared off a crackling song. He couldn't make out the words until midway through the song. Kravitz's "Are You Gonna Go My Way" felt caustic. "*How appropriate!*" he thought as he nonchalantly swung to the lyrics blaring through. Then the morning reveille blasted outside of his bedroom. He tapped the snooze button in the middle of the song. He sat up and grabbed one of the small orange prescription plastic bottles and opened it. He swallowed two codeine pills, then chugged it down with a glass of water.

He looked into his flip phone with its bold numbers still untarnished. He checked for any messages he may have missed during his wakeful slumber-nothing. He gently closed his eyes and breathed a long sigh. Then he placed it next to his .45-caliber pistol. No phone calls, no e-mails, no voicemail.

He sat on the floor, squatted briefly to stretch and assumed the pushup position and began his usual physical calisthenics. He needed to keep his mind alert and his body in top shape in case he was called in or reassigned to assume his post. He was accustomed to the usual physical training throughout his career.

He ran on the treadmill while watching the morning news. He gave himself a high haircut with a hair clipper. Then he took a brief shower and waited on his sofa. It was early fall, and his daughter's birthday was only a few weeks away. He readied himself, waiting by the phone, snacking on his usual breakfast reading magazines and watching TV from his crusted brown leather sofa.

The apartment was small, quaint, plain, and tidy. Its austere decor revealed a man devoid of worldly possessions. A petite wooden chair juxtaposed next to the sofa stood over the red Persian rug he brought back from Afghanistan. Several magazines piled over a wooden coffee table littered with random water stains from a small army shot glass, a nagging eye-sore he'd repeatedly ignored. He kept staring at the small television screen, zoning out while watching the shopping network and cartoons for hours at a time, snickering at the ostentatious products and mumbling off on a tangent. The TV sat next to a white mantle laden with old photos of his team standing in the desert, clad in full combat gear-toting assault rifles. Several of the men died in Wanat. Their unit insignias leaning over the glass frames served as memento for their valor. Marlon felt alienated being away from his men.

By noon, no phone call came as he sifted through the old mail. Without further distractions, he decided to leave for the grocery store to stock up on boxed lunches and refill his prescription. He turned off the television and forgot to pick up his phone upon his departure; his mind was occupied with haunting visions that kept him awake.

He arrived at an empty parking lot and parked at the farthest spot from the PX. The PX was open but empty, its flickering, pallid fluorescent lights littered the ceiling revealing the scuffed linoleum throughout the store. No one except for several cashiers inside the store stood idly by, waiting to pass time. He browsed through the aisles for snacks, canned goods, and perishable items as he waited to fill his prescription. Nothing seemed to have caught his attention; neither the cashier nor the pharmacist could disrupt the monotony. He was tired and irritable. He found several pieces of *Guns & Ammo* magazines displayed by the bookshelves next to the pharmacy. *"How quaint. Magazines designed to kill next to the pharmacy…in case you needed to be medicated."* He shook his head in disbelief. *"That massacre could have been averted if Framm came in here more frequently."*

He picked up his prescription and departed without uttering a single word to the pharmacist. Realizing that he left his cell phone, he quickly drove off and returned to his apartment. Upon his arrival, he checked and noticed several messages on his voicemail. There were three messages that arrived upon his absence. "This is great. I leave for an hour and miss three phone calls," he bemoaned. Sorely aggravated, he picked up the phone and listened to his voicemail. *"Ugh, where did this come from? Unbelievable!"*

First message was from his battalion commander: "Marlon, Colonel Darak! Come and stop by my office at 1700."

Second message was from his wife: "Marlon, this is…well, you know who this is. Your daughter's birthday is coming up, and she…she wants to hear from you. It'd be nice if you can call us. Please…call home. We need to speak to you, please."

Third message was from Charles: "Marlon, this is your brother. Ummm, I need you to call me…It's about dad."

Marlon ended the call before the message was over, blisteringly annoyed to hear the message.

He tossed the phone down on the sofa, turned on the television and sat down. All the while grumbling profanities for missing calls. Thoughts raced through his mind as he pondered upon the recent messages. The first message was what he longed to hear, but the rest brought him unpleasant news and chagrin. There was no time to waste pondering through his estranged wife's abrupt message and his brother's surprising call. *"I need to focus on the task at hand and sift through the whole incident in Wanat,* he thought. *This may be good news…or bad news. Whatever Darak thought, or might say, should be good."*

Later that afternoon, he reported to battalion command on his battle dress uniform, hoping to hear the good news. As he approached the door, he gathered himself, stood erect, and straightened his attire. He looked at the name plate plastered on the wall adjacent to the wooden door –Lt Col. Matthew Darak–BTN CO 3ᴿᴰ ID FORSCOM.

"Wow! I'm gone for several months, and he gets promoted from captain to lieutenant colonel?" he said, shaking his head in disbelief. *"Matt's a good officer…but two ranks within a year? These pointers must be some sort of hotshots and know someone from the Pentagon. Colonel Darak…wow!"* He knocked on the door.

"Who is it?" the man asked.

"Captain Marlon Coe, reporting as ordered, sir!" he belted out.

"Come in, Captain!"

He opened the door and noticed his commanding officer sitting down behind his desk with his attaché standing to his left, holding paperwork to sign. This was quite an unusual meeting. Marlon expected a warm greeting and a firm handshake between two buddies, but the moment appeared formal.

"Come in, Marlon, have a seat," Matt said, bypassing the usual small talk.

"Sir," Marlon replied and sat down.

"It's good to see you, Marlon. You look good!" Matt complemented.

"Thank you, sir," he replied with exuberance. "I try."

"Looks like you've really kept yourself in good shape?" he asked.

"I have, sir!" he replied confidently.

"Well, thanks for coming in at such an abrupt notice." Matt scribbled on a white piece of paper.

Marlon, quite curious as to the contents of the letter, quietly leaned closer and took a short glance following Darak's hand. His thoughts wandered as Matt completed to scribble his signature and dated the form as an official military notice.

"Coe, I have good news, and I have bad news!" Matt noted in a sobering tone.

His face exhibited an emphatic and solemn expression. "Good news is…I can assign you a new post. Bad news is…You've been called to appear on court to face a military tribunal and give an account for Sergeant Framm's actions after the battle. Framm admitted to his actions based on your verbal order. Colonel Moreo, your former C-O, signed off on the papers. If you sign this, you will face trial by court-martial. If not, you will be relieved with dishonorable discharge to say the least, or potentially face murder charges.' He appeared disgusted of the imprudent news to his subordinate. Darak sighed, 'Coe, the media is all over this, and the politicians want to place the blame on senior command…and to the president. The um…Afghanis.' he cleared his throat. 'They want your head!"

Marlon's face grew flustered, his rage burning within him, his jaws locked and tight. Marlon was shocked to hear the news, but he remained calm, keeping his wits intact. He glanced at his commanding officer momentarily as he leaned back on the leather chair, tapping his fingers on its faded edges. He felt blindsided. He was perplexed to offer any responses. So he took a deep breath and cocked his chin.

Darak pushed the folder in front of him. "You can sign this to accept the charges and face court-martial." Darak's face turned somber, portraying such a deep concern for his subordinate's unfortunate events. "I'm sorry, Coe. This came straight from brass, and there isn't much that I can do to repeal this."

Marlon's face grew somber. "Permission to speak, Sir." Darak nodded. "I'm sure that you did your best, Sir." Marlon replied with a sobering remark, easily growing worried.

"I have assigned a JAG to your case. His name is Major Clay Wellis, and he is aware of your situation and the events that transpired at Wanat. He volunteered to take this case personally,' Darak said. 'Marlon, Wellis' brother was in your unit, his younger stepbrother. Luckily, he came out unscathed." Then Darak leaned back. "A jogger found him sitting at the park bench several months ago. He committed suicide, shot himself, and died that night."

Marlon's eyes turned glossy under his furrowed brow, his lips trembled. "What?" he blurted.

"No one knew, not even his older brother. That's why he wanted to represent you...to help anyone on your unit from such a tragedy."

Marlon closed his eyes briefly and wiped his tears quietly. "I...I know Sergeant Wellis. He was a capable soldier...good kid!"

"I can't assign you to any combat unit based on the evidence to be presented to the upcoming trial. But I can assign you to train our new recruits of the 75th Ranger 3rd Battalion," Darak said, brushing off the unfortunate news in a futile attempt to raise any hopes of resuming his post.

"Sir, permission to speak?" Darak nodded subtly. "Who's in command of my men?"

Darak leaned back and cleared his throat. "Captain Valez, from another team has been assigned to the unit. He's a good and capable leader, Marlon. The men are a bit apprehensive, and he doesn't command the loyalty unlike you earned with the men. But they respect him. He served three tours in Afghanistan, and he's taken personal responsibility for the men's training before they redeploy in two months." Darak added. "Anything else that I can help you with? Anything that I can do to answer your questions?" Darak reached out his hand. "Marlon, you can always reach me at my office...Anything you need, anything at all, don't hesitate to call me. Major Wellis will be in contact with you, and he will get all the proper documentation to dismiss the charges." he nodded confidently.

Darak stood up and walked over to him. Marlon followed suit gripping his brown beret, and pinching the creases along the edges. Darak shook his hand. "Good luck, Captain. I pray that you will get through these difficult times. I'm confident that you will be reassigned to a new combat unit once this trial is over. I'll recommend you for battle commission when this mess blows over."

Marlon nodded then saluted. "Sir!" Darak saluted in return.

He proceeded to exit the dark office. He stood outside the door in utter confusion.

The current situation and the past vexed him. "*Article 92*," he thought. "*I followed orders and made the best decision at the time.*" He looked down and closed his eyes for a short moment, slightly anxious of the events to come. "*What just happened?*" With a deep sigh, he opened his eyes, cocked his back, and walked confidently as he exited the building.

He sat down in his car, angrily held on to the steering wheel with both hands, and remained silent for a short period as he surmised the upcoming trial. "Ahh!" he screamed and threw the phone on the chair. "*What did I do to deserve this?*" he thought. '*I did my job, I completed my mission as ordered. How dare they? I gave my whole life, gave up my family to protect my men and lead them to victory! But how could they? They'll never understand. They weren't there. They didn't see the whole thing! Damn! I wouldn't be in this ugly place…this godforsaken fight if I stayed inside. That should have been me! Rick's dead because of me. It should've been me!*" Tears rolled at the side of his face.

Since that fight at Wanat, Marlon was obsessed with past loss and his decision to leave the dead behind. But it was Framm's murderous rampage that consumed him. Past inherited grief saturated his state of being. He was adamant to face the grieving widows and the families of the men who died under his watch. He embraced the burden, selfishly acquiescing to the guilt-tearing hopelessness glossing over his purview. The ringing reminder of tragedy haunted him, straining his motor sensory.

The men he lost under his command weighed heavily on his shoulders, and he felt isolated and trapped. He rejected any psychological counseling to fight his demons and find healing. His marriage was failing due to his unquenched thirst for battlefield glory, and his military career has reached the precipice of ruin. As he aged, the chasm grew wider from his estranged young daughter due to his military obligations that involved prolonged deployments at multiple occasions.

After all the sacrifices he made, he faced a grim reality that affected his efforts;

the time that he sacrificed and the life his men gave for his country were gained for naught. The upcoming military tribunal may exonerate him or may derail his entire career.

The outcome of this trial can result with a dishonorable discharge, or worse, a possible federal incarceration for the death of his men and the death of civilians.

Marlon felt his world crashing to an abrupt, hopeless freefall. The feeling of regret and deep remorse hovered over every decision. He grew numb as time passed, and pessimism consumed his daily affairs, plunging him into lapses of melancholy. He embraced routine, and the thought of losing was unbearable. He wanted to let things go, but losing his men was a scar that would not fade. He couldn't seem to comprehend his unstable emotional state often leading to spurts of rage. And the upcoming trial of his life was fast approaching. Yet something amiss continued to haunt him. The thought of leaving a legacy for his young daughter and his men gave him a sense of purpose, a coup de grâce to break the endless cycle of hopelessness inherited from a painful, dark past.

This notion of leaving a noble legacy kept him sane, that sooner or later, his plight will fade and his moment of glory would be revived. There was a slight inkling of hope, a sense of pride that kept his dark days from overtaking him. This trial, after all, does not define his identity with his men. Honor mattered to him, and he felt that this unraveling setback may be his greatest challenge, yet it may also be his final exoneration from such an elusive closure.

He remained reclusive for several days, staying within the confines of his apartment keeping the lights off, the television on, and his curtains shut. His demeanor displayed clear indifference. He needed to wait for his attorney. There was no other recourse but to wait. He abhorred every passing day, eagerly awaiting for the status of the upcoming trial. His orders to appear in court indicated that he had a few weeks to prepare before the initial query conducted by a committee of senior officers solidifies. And he refused to call Major Wellis, fearing to hear unwanted news that could trigger anxiety attacks. He craved solace; a respite from reality, but it was temporary—neither the pills nor counseling could suppress the past. It seemed that only the bullet could release him from utter hopelessness chafing over his sanity.

It was late afternoon when his cell phone rang. He couldn't recognize the phone number. He assumed that this was the call he was expecting from Major Wellis.

He wanted to answer the phone, but he was afraid to hear the bad news. The ringtone gave a sound of an old dial. It rung five times before his voicemail activated. So, he ignored it until it stopped. He preferred to hear it from his voicemail. When the call ended, he hesitated for a brief moment and slowly pressed the buttons on his phone and listened to his voicemail.

"Marlon. This is Charles. I've been trying to reach you for several days, and I really need you to call me the moment you get this message." There was a brief pause. "It's about dad. I haven't heard from you, and I assumed that you got my message and picked him up! Call me as soon as you get this. I want to know if Pops is okay. 317-509-0580…Call me!"

"What! Dad's here? Why would he be here? I never asked him to visit. This is a joke! This is quite unusual for Charles to make a stupid, sick joke!"

He waited to return the call. For several hours, he moseyed around the living room, watching television to keep his mind occupied. He gave no credence to the message, and he felt it was a nuisance against a pressing issue of his upcoming trial. But something within him couldn't resist the thought of his father's arrival. *"If he was already here, why isn't he here?"* he thought. *'Should he be here by now? If he took the plane, he would have at least called when he landed at the airport. But why isn't he here? Why hasn't he called? Is this Charles's way of saying hello?"*

He brushed the notion of his brother's abrupt phone call and decided to go to sleep. But despite his medications, despite his grogginess, he couldn't avoid thinking about the phone call. After a couple of hours of futile attempt to sleep, he picked up the phone and called his brother. The phone rang a couple of times.

"Hello?" the woman answered.

"Hi. Darcy?" Marlon answered with a rough voice. He paused and cleared his throat. "Hi…this is Marlon."

"Marlon? Is that really you?" Darcy asked with a jovial tone.

"Yeah…it's me," he answered, a bit hesitant.

"It's so good to hear from you. How are you? How's Cheryl? And your daughter?"

A bit dumbfounded by the query, he wondered if his brother knew about his failing marriage and his estranged daughter.

"They…they're good." he answered. "And you? How are you doing?" There was a long pause. Marlon held the phone without uttering any further, hoping to pivot from such awkward conversation.

"I'm doing well. The kid is doing well."

Marlon was aloof, seeking no further reciprocity. There was a silence on both ends and neither one wanted to carry on the conversation. Marlon hesitated, and after an awkward silence, he decided to speak.

"Is…is…Charles there?"

"Oh, Charles? Yes, he just returned. He's preparing for his sermon this Sunday. Hold on, okay? Let me get him on the line."

She walked briskly to the large study room to bring the phone to her husband, who was immersed in front of his laptop, typing his upcoming sermons, completely fixated at every word of the letter. She handed him the phone and whispered "Marlon" to his ear. But he was too distracted from his work that he failed to heed his wife's prodding.

"This is Reverend Charles," he answered with firm, confident voice.

Marlon paused briefly, hesitant to reply.

"Hello!" Charles asked sternly.

Marlon sensed his petulant, impatient tone. "Charles, its Marlon."

"Hey," Charles responded nonchalantly. 'Did you get my messages?"

"Yes," Marlon replied. He was a bit annoyed at his brother's bluntness. 'What do you mean Dad's coming?"

"Did you pick him up?" Charles asked, a bit perturbed.

"No."

"Marlon, listen and listen carefully," Charles said with condescending tone. "I called you two days ago and left a message that he's on his way there. If he's not there, he's probably waiting for you at the station."

"Station…What station?" Marlon retorted.

By now, Charles had realized that their father may still be waiting to be fetched. "Yes! Train station."

"The train station is at least five hours from here, Charles," Marlon replied. "Why the train station?"

"You have to pick him up, Marlon. That's why I called you…but apparently you didn't listen!" he scoffed.

"This is not the right time, Charles." Marlon bristled and made a deep, quiet sigh. Marlon felt being goaded into a futile argument.

"Go, pick him up! He was supposed to arrive last night," Charles asserted.

"Why the train? Can't you afford a plane ticket? You should have called me before you sent him over. I could have bought him a plane ticket!" Marlon replied angrily.

"Oh Please." Charles breathed deeply. "Go, pick him up!"

"What's his cell phone number?"

"Write this down, 5-1-2-2-8-0-0-5-8-0," Charles replied. "Did he call you?"

"No, the only message that I got was from you and from Cindy."

"Call him. Let me know after you pick him up," Charles said, eager to end the call.

"All right. I'll call him on the way!" Marlon hung up the phone.

He immediately stood up from the bed, grabbed his worn-out blue Cedarville College sweatshirt from the closet, and pulled it over his trousers. He picked up his light-brown military-issued jacket and a set of keys. He grabbed his cell phone and wallet from the laminated countertop and walked over to the door. He looked around to ensure that all the lights were off and the drapes shut. Then he exited and locked the door behind him. After several steps, he returned to the door and made sure it was locked. "No one enters, no one leaves," he whispered.

Chapter Four

The trip from Fort Bragg to Atlanta took approximately six hours. Due to his father's deteriorating physical condition, Marlon needed to reach the station before midnight, fearing for his father's safety and his volatile temperament. Any train station offered little comfort to any unwitting visitors. His father suffered from dimentia and Parkinson's disease; a degenerative condition that subdues the mind and debilitates the senses. His psychological state has been ebbing for the past seven years due to his late stage dementia that further complicates his plight. The illness had worsened over the years as the physical signs of dementia grew more evident. Marlon found out about his father's condition eight years earlier during his first tour in Iraq just right before his mother's death.

He took to the highway with his 2003 white Chevy pickup, blazing on the right lane, avoiding close proximity to the median guardrail. The cracks and potholes kept him nervous and cautious; the visual threats of improvised explosive devises buried beneath the cracked surface remained fresh and vivid. He'd seen too many men maimed and killed from IEDs in the streets of Baghdad. To keep his mind occupied, he turned on the radio, blasting the volume to alert his senses and fight grogginess.

It's been years since Marlon had seen his father. The traumatic physical and emotional abuse at the hands of an alcoholic father inflamed painful memories that spurred deep resentment, a festering wound inherited from his childhood past that haunted him despite his father's absence. During his childhood, his absentee father, resentful of his job and his mounting debt, frequented a louche establishment nearby. He worked straight through the day and came home late at night—inebriated, careless, and belligerent, causing ruckus that echoed through the neighbors' doorsteps. His obnoxious dispensation was only heightened by cheap whiskey. When the bottle ran dry, his cantankerous nature and guilt turned violent—often at the expense of the boys.

For Marlon, childhood memories were difficult and irrepressible; the bliss and innocence of his youth was far and few. He remembered the lost days when he and his brother spent a stint with their sobered father. And one of the fondest memories that he recalled was the day when his father treated them to a movie theater to watch an old Western. Summoning the memories of any blissful occasions was almost as painful as revisiting the hurt-filled youth. Incidents full of harsh discipline clouded his thoughts and scarred him throughout his adulthood.

As he drove through, he recalled one early Saturday morning, right after his fifteenth birthday. The eventful day turned sour when his father, a man with deep, booming voice, dragged him for several miles to visit the local strip mall to beg for a job from every store manager. This occurred in broad daylight at the sight of his peers. Being a timid, shy teenager, he barely held the confidence to ask strangers for favors as he was physically threatened by his father to collect every single employment application from all twenty-five retail stores. For Marlon, this brought tremendous angst. Several times, his father, tipsy from chugging old whiskey, slapped him over the head whenever he left the store empty-handed. He recalled the embarrassing moments in front of other people and several teenagers gawking as they passed by, crying from the pressure and humiliation ascending from fear. For Marlon, these indelible moments etched in his psyche had deepened, and the chasm grew wider between them. He barely reminisced of the wonderful days he spent with his father, but he was far remove from the past fraught with traumatic upbringing. Marlon is convinced that his father's rage greatly diminished his confidence and inflamed his vulnerability.

Speeding through the dark, empty highway, he was immediately spotted by highway patrol car who clocked him for speeding. Marlon noticed the patrol officer to his left, and by the time, he pumped the brakes, the officer had already turned on his sirens, a clear signal to pull over. Marlon was a bit surprised but unfazed. For him, this only prolonged his time-sensitive trip, but he was accustomed to surprises, and this inconvenient, unwanted occasion felt trivial in comparison to stressful encounters. He refused to acquiesce further to such flammable circumstance. He focused on task in order to ensure a safe, peaceful arrival of his father. As he pulled to the right shoulder, the patrol car pulled right behind him with its lights flashing blatantly, illuminating the dark road for a far distance. The red and blue streaks rolling above the brown Crown Victoria revealed an imposing man stepping out of the car and calmly approaching his truck.

The patrol officer, an older Caucasian, clean cut and formal, cautiously approached the right side of his vehicle instead of the driver side; he appeared suspicious and cocky, easing his right hand over the handle of his sidearm. Then he pointed his black twelve-inch flashlight directly straight on Marlon's face. His suede, faded hat barely touched his eyebrows; its state emblem pinned in the middle glistened from the flashing lights behind the truck bed. Darkness revealed only a shadow that hovered over his eyes, with its silhouette revealing only the outline of his face. The bill of his hat filtered the light over his face. The white of his eyes glistened as they remain fixated at the man sitting behind the steering wheel; they appeared pernicious, and his face was devoid of any emotions. The officer knocked on the side window, spinning his fingers. Marlon hesitated momentarily but obliged. He grew slightly agitated at the obnoxious light pointed straight at his eyes. He glanced away from its glare as he kept both hands on the wheel. The officer came up right to his door, glancing inside the vehicle as he greeted him.

"Good evening!" the officer bellowed.

Marlon was bit perturbed from such inconvenience. "Evening, Officer!"

"License and registration," the officer asserted.

"Yes…um…one sec. Let me pull it from the glove compartment."

He slowly pulled his driver's license and the vehicle registration card along with his insurance card and slowly handed it to the man.

After a examining his ID and his insurance registration card, the man noticed the expired date.

"Your insurance has expired!" he scoffed.

"It is? I just renewed my insurance last month. They…they were supposed to send me a new one. You can look it up and call my insurance company."

The officer reciprocated with a chastising stare. He took his papers without hesitation. He snagged the papers right from his hand then turned towards his vehicle.

"Wait here!" he said as he galumphed to his cruiser.

As time slowly passed, Marlon grew impetuous—annoyed at the man's conscious delay and blatant disregard for his errand. He was confident that the man would recognize his military ID and exonerate him, and perhaps to thank him for his military service. Then several police cruisers heading west whizzed by them.

Marlon was surprised to see the officer taking his time, checking for any incriminating objects on the cargo bed. After several minutes, the officer got out of his car and walked on the driver side of the vehicle. He leaned down and handed him the insurance card along with a yellow traffic ticket. The officer never hesitated or paused to ascertain the pursuit.

He did not utter a word. He simply looked at Marlon with a straight face and trotted back to his cruiser.

"Sir," the man expressed bluntly, "do you know why I pulled you over?"

"I'm sorry, Officer, I wasn't really paying attention to my speed. But I'll slow down this time -I promise," he answered politely.

"You were going seventy miles per hour on a sixty-five-mile-an-hour speed limit. You're lucky your insurance checked out," the man scolded.

"Oh, I uh…I didn't realize that. You'll have to excuse me if I drove too fast. See, I was on my way to pick up my father in Atlanta. I tried to stay within the limits, Officer. But can I just get a warning this time?"

The officer glanced at him and smirked as he handed him a yellow receipt. "Well, here's the citation. Here's the fine. Make sure that you appear in court, or a warrant will be issued against you," he asserted.

"Oh, thank you. I guess the warning is out of the question, huh?" he replied with a smug look.

The man pointed his finger. "You people should know better than to ask for more favors!" He smirked, shaking his head, "Unbelievable!" He looked straight at him with disgust. "Don't let me see you here again speeding! Do you understand me?"

"Yes, sir! Roger that!" Marlon replied as he rolled up his window and tossed the ticket on the seat. He turned on the ignition and left. This unwanted nuisance and stressful event further delayed his trip. The patrol car immediately drove off ahead of him.

Half an hour later, he drove into a crime scene; it was a highway shooting. He calmly navigated through three patrol cars blocking both lanes—its doors ajar and its lights flashing blindly. On the left side of the road, near the median, he noticed a state patrol officer hastening to resuscitate the injured officer lying on the pavement. The victim's light-gray uniform was stained crimson red as he bled profusely from several gunshot wounds on his torso and inner thigh. Marlon's instincts immediately kicked in. He pulled over the middle of the highway several feet behind the nearest patrol car, lit several flares he found at the back of his truck and proceeded to assist the officer at the side of the road. He noticed a white Crown Victoria with tinted windows pulled to the right shoulder several feet in front of the first patrol car; its sides were riddled with bullets, and the driver side door was missing. Marlon noticed the young black man brandishing a TEC-9 semiautomatic weapon on his right hand. He was lying lifeless in between the car door and the driver seat. His blood dripped from his right cheek, soaking his white shirt. His head was tilted to the side and his mouth was agape—hopelessly gasping for air. His chest was convulsing. He sported a red baseball cap with stitched emblem. Marlon knew that there was nothing he could do to save the boy. Within seconds, he succumbed to his wounds and died just as the fourth patrol car arrived at the scene.

Marlon couldn't spare any further delay and rushed to aid the officer holding the wounded man lying on the pavement. As he ran to the wounded officer, the thick smell of gunpowder grew intoxicating.

"Can I help, Officer?" he shouted confidently, but the man didn't answer. He was taking over the radio pinned to his right shoulder. Again he asked firmly, "Officer! Can I help?"

The officer, still shocked, looked up and gave a blank stare, seeing an imposing man standing in front of him. He hesitated for a moment, then nodded at Marlon. "Come here and help me stop this bleeding!" the officer replied The victim lay helplessly flat on his back. A bullet pierced cleanly through his left shoulder, just inches above his vest. Another bullet was lodge through his left thigh. The man started dozing off, his blood splattered on the gray asphalt.

Marlon's instinct kicked in-he took his belt buckle and tightly tied it around the man's left thigh using it as a tourniquet to save the man's life. Then he took his jacket and bundled it behind the man's head to keep his head up and keep him from losing consciousness. He took off his sweater and placed it under the man's left shoulder to elevate the injured side and reduce the bleeding. He noticed the man's face as he pressed both hands on his left shoulder. It was the same officer who pulled him from the side of the road. He never thought much of the man and the treatment he received. Instead, he focused on stopping the bleeding. The other officer was standing by the side of his patrol car, shocked to see the chaotic scene, was frantically relaying messages over the radio- pleading for a helicopter rescue. Marlon remained calm under duress-unfazed by the chaos around him as he worked on the injured man. The bleeding began to stop on the man's thigh, but he was dozing off due to blood loss. Marlon noticed him grasping a Glock pistol with his right hand which got him worried. He remained cautious of the man's intent-the man may unwittingly shoot him for his appearance. He looked at the man's brass nametag –Swift.

"Officer Swift! Listen to me. You're bleeding badly, but help is on way," he assured him as he continued to press on with both hands on his left shoulder. "Help is on the way. Stay with me, okay?" He smiled tapping him by the shoulder.

The man smiled cordially as he remained quiet and calm.

"Listen! Do you have first aid with you?"

The man pointed with his right hand. "Left...left side...pouch." he coughed.

Marlon quickly reached out and grabbed his right hand. "I need your hand.' The man obliged and nodded. 'Press your shoulder firmly, right here. Don't let go!"

Marlon then grabbed the small first-aid kit from his belt and opened it. He took the morphine syringe and injected him below the sternum. "It's going to be all right, Officer, you'll make it. Just stay with me and don't go to sleep, okay!"

The man nodded slowly.

After several minutes, the first ambulance arrived. The crew immediately worked to rescue Officer Swift. One of the crew looked at Marlon as he stood up, completely amazed at what he had done to stop the bleeding.

The second ambulance arrived at the scene to tend to the other victim. There was not much that they could do to resuscitate the young man.

They gently placed his body on a black body bag and loaded him on the second ambulance. As they took his body, Marlon noticed an opened bottle of whiskey on the driver seat. He also noticed several prescription drug containers and stacks of cash scattered all over the floor of the car. He slowly approached the car and noticed the bottles were labeled with Oxycontin.

Another State Patrol officer came over and tapped him over the shoulder. "You can't stay here, sir! This is a crime scene."

Marlon glanced over and noticed the officer. "Yes…of course." He glanced back at the man and hesitated, "Anything I can do to help?"

"Did you witness the whole incident?" the officer asked.

"No, I just got here after the shooting. I came and helped Officer Swift."

"Well, we're good here, but I will need your phone number in case we need to call you for further info."

"Yes, sure, it's 9-0-8-5-1-2-7-7-1-5."

"Thanks!' the officer replied, "Oh, before you go, how did you know how to stop the bleeding? Seems you have done this before." The man looked at the tourniquet. "You did a great job saving this man's life, how'd you know what to do?"

"A lifetime of military service…75th Rangers, 2nd Battalion. I'm also a Green Beret," he replied.

The man's eyes widened. "What a miracle! This man owes you his life. If it wasn't for your quick thinking, he would have bled to death,"

"Well, it's the least I can do for his service,' Marlon replied confidently. 'You good now?"

"I think we're good. Well, I can't thank you enough. You're a hero."

"It's cool. Anytime!" Marlon smiled as he walked back to his vehicle and looks at one of the medic tending Swift. "Take care of him. I'm sure he'll live."

"Yeah, he's stable. We'll load him up and take him to the ER," the medic replied. Another officer who arrived at the scene walked over to Marlon and shook his hand. "Thanks a bunch! You're a real hero."

Marlon nodded in reply.

"You know, we could really use someone like you in the force," he said as Marlon entered his truck.

Marlon glanced over, hesitated briefly, and nodded. "Thank you… means a lot."

He turned the ignition and drove off. The noble and heroic deed brought about a sense of haughtiness. And the rush of adrenaline was intoxicating. The sudden thrust of invincibility felt liberating. It was the closest feeling of being in the battlefield, but the jolt was short-lived. As he drove on the empty road, the vivid memories of past exploits were reignited. It brought him back to a place and a time when his men rallied behind his lead; a time when he was once venerated. But the past was long gone; a past he relished and he refused to abdicate. The momentary silence projected a past of faded glory; a fragmented memento of solace that only corroded his judgement.

The whole incident took a bit longer than he had anticipated. He knew that he had deviated from his initial plan, much to his father's chagrin for to such blatant tardiness. But he felt numb, bent on neglecting his father's needs. He was resentful, clearly apathetic to his brother's plea. The train station was still hours away, but he was in no rush to accommodate. After all, this was a last-minute effort that came at an unfortunate event. For him, as long as he arrived, regardless of time, his father deserved the treatment, an implied contempt for their plea, and a passive feeling of entitlement for his father's offenses. He was not to be sullied any further; he was in charge, in control, and unapologetic.

Saving the life of a police officer gave him a sense of purpose and significance.

He was ecstatic to be involved with such a tragic incident. The bleeding man incited lucid memories of the past, conjuring a heightened sense of fear in the midst of a firefight. The smell of gunpowder, the morbid scene and life teetering on the edge triggered an adrenaline kick that awakened a violent past buried deep within his psyche. He couldn't shake the memories, and he refused to ignore it. It became a place of comfort, cocooned within the darkness of his plight.

It was two o'clock in the morning when he arrived at the terminal. He noticed that the doors were locked. So, he trotted up to the terminal and peered from outside the windows. The halls were illuminated brightly by several fluorescent lights hanging under the vaulted ceiling. He kept searching for any passengers, but no one was around. He strolled around the stone building to the back to see if there were anyone present who may have seen his father. The train schedule posted on the back wall revealed that the last train arrived ten o'clock. The next train would not be arriving until the following morning. He sat on the bench at the side of the train tracks for several minutes, biding his time hoping for his father to appear. But no one appeared. To his chagrin, he stood up and turned and returned to his vehicle, then he noticed a man sweeping the steps outside the door. He approached him and waved his hand. He greeted the man with a slight nod. The old man was quite tall; his face was devoid of any wrinkles, and his hair revealed a man who lived for many seasons. "Sir! Pardon me, but have you seen an old black man waiting inside the station?" he asked.

The man momentarily hesitated then shook his head.

"No? Okay, um…has anyone asked you for directions? Say, an old man?"

"What are you doing here?" The man replied softly.

"What do you mean…I just asked you if you've seen an old black man?" Marlon replied.

The old man looked at him with a solemn face. Marlon scoffed. "Never mind…you obviously don't understand," flailing his hand as he began to walk away.

"I completely understand. But my question to you is, where are you going?" The man gently replied.

Marlon turned around to answer his unusual question. "I'm here to… Sir? Where are you?" The man had disappeared before he could answer.

"Huh, pretty fast for an old man," he thought. "Well, I'm here 'cause I'm looking for my old man. Have you seen him?" he yelled, hoping that the man could hear him. "Thank you!" He shouted as he walked briskly back to his vehicle.

He sat and waited quite a bit inside his vehicle while repeatedly checking his watch. By the seventh time he gazed at his watch, it was past three in the morning. He slowly closed his eyes and fell asleep.

Chapter Five

"Medic!" he hollered but no one responded. He called out for a medic several times but his calls were drowned out by the constant barrage of gunfire. For several minutes, he held tightly on to his radioman until the medic came to rescue him. Marlon desperately called out to him to keep him alive, but the young man struggled to stay awake; fading in and out of consciousness.

Robben was clinging to every breath; his eyes twitched uncontrollably and his pupils were dilated. His right arm was severed, and he was losing more blood. He was in utter shock and in a complete daze. The medic applied the tourniquet and injected the morphine in hopes to resuscitate him, but they couldn't keep his blood pressure from crashing. Unable to stop the bleeding, Robben instinctively panted for air. Then his convulsions slowly eased as he drew his last breath. His head sank and his mouth was open, his eyes had closed and his skin turned cold. He was gone. Marlon's feeble attempt to resuscitate the young man was futile.

This was Gracen Robben's first tour of duty in Afghanistan. He was given a short leave to return to his family, but he refused it. Instead, he chose to stay and offered his leave for another teammate whose young wife gave birth to their first child. He served in the 110th Mountain Division and was assigned to fill in for Sergeant Brown, Marlon's radioman. Marlon's team grew fond of the young upstart in a short time. His quick wit, dry sarcasm, and idealistic naiveté endeared him to the team. He was only eighteen when enlisted right after high school. Gracen graduated top of his high school class. He led his baseball team to a state championship as team captain during his junior year. He was offered several scholarships to attend Princeton, Stanford, and Duke in hopes to become a chemical engineer, but he chose to enlist and join the army to carry on the family tradition in hopes to follow his grandfather's footsteps and forge his own heroic ventures. Gracen was deeply enamored by his grandfather's legendary exploits as an elite army sniper during the Korean War. His romanticized war stories cultivated Gracen's desire to follow in his footsteps despite of his parent's objections. Gracen joined the infantry, and two years later he was deployed in Afghanistan then assigned as Marlon's de facto radioman thrusting him into one of the most hazardous provinces in Afghanistan.

Marlon tried to remain calm, but the intense firefight and the gravity of his concussion impaired his instincts. The distress calls for help from the injured and the chaos brought by the fog of war intensified further as the enemy began a relentlessly coordinated assault. They were caught in a vice against a larger force that was well dug in from the hilltops. To the detriment of his team, further reinforcement was delayed. He kept his focus regardless of the confusion to make sure that his men would survive until help arrived.

The medic came and attended to the young man checking his vitals on his wrist and his neck but found no pulse as Marlon held him tightly.

"Cap! Let go! I got this!" the medic shouted. "Sir! Can you hear me? Captain Coe!"

Marlon awoke to a sudden lightning strike. The obnoxious sound of heavy rain struck the windshield violently. Slowly, he glanced over the side of the vehicle, and checked his wristwatch. "Five o'clock," he muttered as he sat up. A bit groggy, he shook his head quickly and wiped his face with both knuckles. He took his coat, stained with spots of blood and flipped the neck collar over his head. He opened the door and jogged over to the entrance. The lights were on, but no one was inside. His father was nowhere to be found, and the old man was gone. After a brief search, he rushed back to his pickup truck and dried his wet hair from the rain. He waited for several minutes, then picked up his cell phone.

"*He's not gonna like this,*" he thought as he scrolled up his call history and pushed the call button on his phone.

After the phone rang several times, he pressed the end button. He looked on his phone, scrolled down further on his call history to see if any calls came in during his sleep, but none arrived since his last phone call to his brother. He sighed deeply, slightly perturbed—feeling the weight of inconvenience.

Chapter Six

He stood inside the train terminal, gazing at the train schedule, fervently searching for the right departure time for a particular destination. The letters and numbers hastily posted on the black board hanging above the ticket booth appeared convoluted. His eyes, weak and fading, bounced to and fro, searching for any right word or hint that may appear familiar, perhaps to jog his memory back. He fielded a blank stare, confused at the board saturated with small letters in strewn in random order. He was slightly leery and growing anxious, unable to piece it together. And his worn-out brown leather suitcase grew heavy. His shoulders ached, and his right arm was numbed from pulling the weight. He stood there motionless for quite some time, waiting for an answer.

"Raleigh, North Carolina. Seven o'clock. Am I supposed to head to North Carolina? Or is it Atlanta, Georgia...or is it Savannah, Georgia? This is one complicated board, for such a simple method of transportation," he thought.

His eyebrows raised, wrinkling his freckled forehead. He tipped his fedora to ease the tension from his calvous head. Its white lining stained with years of sweat concealed what remained of his peppered gray hair. His eyes appeared tiresome and lonely, his nape bent, his gullet flapped, and his shoulders sagged. Years of hard drinking hastened his aging over time that left distinct lines above his cheek bones. For years, he has struggled to tilt his shoulders back, and his strength was ebbing. His posture revealed a man weary and obscure.

He kept staring at the board, standing alone, hoping to piece all the clues; anxiously hoping for someone to aid him. He was losing all inkling of comprehension for his intended destination. As he lingered through the day, people at the terminal kept passing by, heading to their intended destination without noticing. Slowly, his feet grew sore and his knees began to buckle.

He didn't notice three young men who appeared behind him. They wore saggy clothes, sporting dark blue designer jeans that hung precariously beneath their waist. Their basketball jerseys beneath their large, thick coats barely concealed their colorful tattoos etched randomly on their chest and neck. They seemed to relish the attention from the people waiting at the station.

At first, they failed to notice the old man as they passed by. When they walked by, one of the boys intentionally bumped him from the back. The old man felt a sudden, violent shove. The boy looked at the the old man and gave him an angry stare. The old man remained oblivious, clearly preoccupied with the schedule and paid no heed to their intrusion. The boys were taller than him and displayed some mischievous behavior. Their shaved head and long goatees separately braided by pieces of colorful hairbands stood out from the crowd and each passenger steered clear from their path. The boys seemed to revel on the incident, slowly approached him.

The boy leaned closer with his hands inside his pockets and his teeth biting his lower lip. His eyes, burning in anger, locked on the tip of his hat. The others were quite bemused and kept an angry stare as the boy inched closer. He sized up the old man, who seemed timid and helpless, and grabbed him man's on his sleeves, his eyes shifted and locked on to his.

"What are you staring at, old man!"

The old man, still confused, did not reply. He pulled his collar back and slowly backed away, hoping to avoid any confrontation.

The other young men, seething in anger, clinched their fists tightly, ready to strike at any moment. "What's your problem? You got a problem, pops?" one of the young man yelled.

The boy, with his hand on the old man's sleeve, pulled him off the ground. "What you staring at?" he scolded.

Then others began to snicker, taunting the old man to fight. Several people waiting nearby began to take notice of this commotion, but no one interceded for the hapless old man.

"Is there a problem here?" a powerful, commanding voice boomed from the crowd. Everyone stopped and looked around to see who it was. "I said, is there a problem here?"

The boys suddenly stopped and glanced around to see if anyone was bold enough to interfere with their shenanigans. The crowd parted to the sides and a very tall police officer calmly walked toward them. His piercing piercing emerald eyes fixated at the man holding the old man. At six-foot four, the officer, with is uniform and his loaded belt, appeared menacing. His large frame exuded such strong presence that everyone, including the boys, was frightened.

The old man slowly turned his head and glanced at the officer, with his eyes squinting. He was surprised to see an imposing figure, his chiseled face stood out from his dark complexion. As the officer came close, the old man felt a sense of ease; there was a sense of tranquility that eased his racing heart, washing away his fears. The panic melted way under the man's growing shadow.

Without uttering any word at the young men, the officer gave them a stern look—his eyes chastising their nefarious ploy. The young man's face grew flustered, and his fists unclenched as he retreated back with his cohorts.

"Nah, man. We cool, we cool," he mumbled softly, shaking his head nervously.

They quickly backed away and hastened to their train, fearing an arrest. The old man felt liberated and cocky as he stood proudly, quietly basking on the rising cheer of strangers. The officer smiled gently, then he nodded and kept walking, resuming on his usual routine. And he walked away, the old man grew anxious. He wanted to thank him, and perhaps plead for his assistance. He was alone, searching for a way to remember his intended destination. The officer sensed his desperation and turned to him.

"Do you know where you're headed?" the officer asked.

He hesitated. "My son...I was suppose to board a train to meet my son,' he replied shyly. 'See, I have not seen him for quite some time, and I was told that he wanted to see me. That's why I needed to board the train, but I can't recall which destination."

"Do you have a ticket with you?" he asked politely.

"Um, I did, but somehow it got misplaced. Can you help me? I must have placed it somewhere, but I can't seem to remember, strange."

"Let's start with your pockets, shall we?" He smiled. The old man, frantically searching for his ticket on every pocket was embarrassed. "Um, I've searched my pockets," he softly replied. "I'm tellin' you, I ain't got it. It's somewhere in the terminal."

"Do you have a wallet?"

"Yes, I checked there but it ain't there. Can you help me look for it? It could have fell to the floor," he replied, looking pensive.

"Do me a favor. Will you do this for me?" the officer kindly prodded.

"Sure!"

He grabbed his wallet under his right lapel and pulled it in front of the officer to demonstrate a fleeting attempt to satisfy the man's requests. Then he handed him his wallet.

"Okay, it looks like you have a ticket here.' He glanced at the ticket. 'And from what it says here, it appears that you just missed the train."

The old man's face grew flustered, slightly dumbfounded. "You found my ticket?"

"Yes, it's right here. It says Atlanta, Georgia."

The old man nodded innocently, his anxious expression grew obvious.

"I'm not going to Atlanta!" he quibbled.

"The ticket says you do." the officer kindly replied and handed him the ticket. "Never mind that. You missed your train." The officer smiled. "Now, how in the world did you end up here in Meridian, Mississippi?" Eli gave him a blank stare. "I actually went out to grab something to eat. When I came back, the train was gone.' Eli replied in shame. 'You can't stop the train once it leaves."

"What do you suppose I do now, sir?" the old man asked, pulling his hat down.

"You will have to take the next train, which is leaving tomorrow morning."

"Tomorrow?' He paused and shook his head in disbelief. "Tommorow... Man!"

He looked up. "Isn't there another train coming in soon? I mean...I mean, it's still early, isn't it?"

"That's the next train coming in."

"Well, um...what do you suppose I do now?"

"Do you know anyone who lives here in town?"

"No, I've never been to this town, and I'm afraid that I'm alone here."

"There is a small hotel across the street. I can take you there, if that is all right with you."

"I guess. I don't have much of a choice, do I?"

"I'm afraid not," shaking his head. "There's no need for you to stay here. You need to get some sleep and come back fully recuperated."

"I can stay here and wait until the next day."

"You can't stay here but you can rent a hotel room for the night, I'll take you there.

The old man was slightly suspicious. "I don't have a way to return here. I can't afford a taxi."

"Don't you worry about that, I'll bring you back here on time to catch the next train."

"All right, I guess I can go. I can trust you, right?"

The officer replied with a grin, "Yes, you don't have anything to be afraid of. But you will have to trust me. Agreed?"

The old man nodded,

"Here, let me help you," he said, gently prying the suitcase from his hand.

They proceeded to leave together. "I didn't get your name?"

"You can call me Sam," the man replied with a blissful grin.

"Well, it is nice to be of acquaintance with you, Sam. I'm Elijah. You can call me Eli."

"It's a pleasure to meet you, Eli. I know a good friend named Elijah. Quite a bold man, a bit quiet and stoic, but a very wise man," he laughed.

"Yessa! We're the wise ones." Eli grinned politely.

The two men walked out of the terminal into the squad car parked at the side of the gutter right by the entrance of the terminal.

"I know that you must be hungry, Eli. Let me buy you dinner," the officer asserted.

"Um...I'm sorry, but I don't have any money left with me. Just enough to buy another ticket," he relented timidly.

"Do you always turn down a stranger's offer?" He chuckled.

"No, no, no. I just don't have much money...that's all."

"Well, I did not ask you to buy dinner, did I?" the officer asked innocently.

"No, no, Officer, you're too kind."

"Eli, the hotel is right across the street and the diner is a just a couple of blocks away."

Eli hesitated as he sat on the backseat. The officer, quite amused at the man's naiveté, chucked. "Eli, you're not my suspect, and I'm not your chauffer. Don't go there! We're not going to the station. Come up here by the front seat. It's much warmer."

He took off his fedora and held it near his chest as a gesture of respect. "Oh, sorry Officer, pardon me." He paused and closed the back door. He peeked over on the front side window as the officer rolled the window down. "Are you sure it's okay to sit up here?' he asked, quite surprised of the man's overtly kind gesture. 'I don't want to impose."

"It's okay, Eli. I am officially off the clock. I'm just a regular person helping a friend. That's all…if that is okay with you."

Eli sat comfortably at the front-a foregone memory of his youth where he once found himself at the backseat of a patrol car on its way to the city jail due to public intoxication. He noticed the laptop mounted on the middle console and the shotgun hoisted and locked juxtaposed to the side of the computer next to the glove box. He looked around as the officer rolled up the windows and started the engine.

"My treat!" the officer blurted. "I'm sure that you're going to be a great company. I would love to hear your stories."

"*Stories? Can I really trust this man? I mean…he's white!*" He sat straight up as he buckled his seat belt to ensure that he followed the rules to avoid a reprimand from the lawman.

Elijah Coe grew up in Georgia at the height of the civil rights movement. He had witnessed the injustice imposed on blacks being treated as second-class citizens. Racism was prevalent throughout the South in the fifties and sixties. Overt segregation and injustice that African Americans suffered were common. He'd heard the racial slurs and witnessed the blatant insult. He had endured racial discrimination in restaurants, public facilities, and churches. He had tasted racial inequality and the subversive efforts to repress basic human rights of black people throughout his lifetime. The blatant injustices at the hands of local officials and law enforcement remained unchecked. The civil rights movement that sparked the protests led by black protestant preachers left an indelible impression that fueled a sense of pride and deep-rooted resentment, mistrusting the establishment. He was resentful, scorned throughout his adulthood. He was convinced that the prejudices that existed remains pervasive and strong even after sixty years of desegregation. He was reserved, doubtful, and suspicious of whites, cynical at every opportunity that arose. The race issue greatly tilted his perception.

His glances randomly landed on the man's face with bewilderment, unable to conceive the kindness offered to him by a stranger—one with pasted skin color wearing a badge and a gun. He was leery of the man's kind gesture, and his cynical thoughts kept him aloof. After a long, awkward silence he opened a dialogue.

"Sir, I don't have any money to pay for dinner."

The man nodded in reply. "You told me that. Why don't you allow me the kind gesture?"

They arrived at the front diner with no one else present on the empty lot. "Here's the diner! You'll love their soup. They make this great clam chowder that makes you want to come back for more," he said in a jovial tone.

"I love clam chowder!" he mumbled.

"Good! I'm sure you'll be more satisfied after tonight. This soup will change your life," he said confidently.

The diner was located several blocks from the terminal. It had been in business for several decades serving patrons from all walks of life that passed through the small terminal. Eli noticed that the diner was empty. No one except for the waitress was present, yet the restaurant remained open. She was the last one who manned behind the counter, waiting to close for the night. They came in and sat by the edge behind the counter.

"Are you still serving?" the offer smiled.

"That's right. We're open for business for another hour. Ain't by choice, if you ask me," she replied without looking up while she swept the floor.

"Good! My friend and I would like to have some of your delicious clam chowder!" he blurted with excitement.

Eli stood behind him waiting to be ushered and seated.

The waitress gave him a stern look and shook her head. "Well, you can sit anywhere you want. I'll be right with you."

She placed the broom behind the counter, slightly annoyed at the last-minute guests and handed them a menu.

The officer rubbed his hands with glee. "Thank you, but this will not be necessary." He looked at Eli. "My friend here and I would like to try your soup...the best kind, and a glass of your sweat tea." He looked at the old man and smiled. "You will thank me for this."

Eli was not impressed. No soup could surpass the recipe of his late wife-the kind of soup that brought blissful ecstasy. He whipped out his wallet from his side right pocket and noticed he has only two dollars.

"Oh no, I got this! You're money is no good here," the officer replied.

"Oh! No! I don't mind," the old man replied. "You've helped me more than enough. At least...let me return the favor."

"Well, that's very generous of you, Elijah," he replied with a wide smile.

The old man nodded clasping his hands together as he rested his elbows over the countertop. He remained quiet for several minutes while wearing a somber face. The two men glanced at the TV hanging on the upper corner of the room. It was blaring off the news from Afghanistan. It was an old, black box that sat on the top shelf; its concave glass tube was covered in dust evident of its age and constant neglect. As the two men looked on, the waitress brought in the hot soup on a white porcelain bowl. The TV played the late-night news; its screen, although fuzzy and crackled, gave just enough clarity for any patron who listened to comprehend the contents.

"In other news today: four soldiers have been reported killed in action in eastern Afghanistan. They were said to have been victims of an IED. These men were part of a Special Forces team sent on a mission in Wanat province where an ongoing battle has ensued with NATO forces fighting against the Taliban."

The officer remained quiet, his face somber. Elijah glanced to his side and noticed the man's sadness.

"You know, my son...he is in the army," Elijah proudly said.

"He's a brave soldier," the officer replied.

"He's been deployed several times in Afghanistan, and he's come home. I'm on my way to see him...I think," he said. The officer felt a sense of doubt and anxiety on his voice.

"You're son has accomplished a lot," he replied with a slight grin.

"I'm very proud of what he's become."

"Does he know that?"

The old man, unsure of his reply, looked down to his soup and took a sip. "I'm not sure," he mumbled.

"When was the last time you told him that you were proud of him?" he prodded.

"I'm not sure, really. See, it's been a while since I've seen him," he paused as he sipped his soup. "'Tis been quite a while," he said, slightly embarrassed.

"Are you not going to see him?"

"Yes, if God allows."

"So, how long has it been?" He looked at him. Elijah closed his eyes as he waddled his spoon in the bowl looking straight on and searching for answers.

"Can't remember, really! It's been a while."

"He must be excited to see you then, is he not?"

Eli smirked. "I guess."

The officer chuckled.

"Why is that funny?" Eli blurted.

"No, no, it's not funny. Just ironic, that's all."

"What do you mean by that?"

"You sound really proud of him, but embarrassed for yourself, why?"

"My son...well, he's not too fond of me!"

Eli leaned over to check on the man's bowl. "Listen, I really like this soup, and it looks like you still haven't touched yours," Eli said.

"Oh! No, please forgive me for prying. I did not mean to..."

"Nah! It's fine. The news...it brings the best of people," he replied sarcastically.

"I'm glad that you told me about your son." Sam leaned back. "What's his name?" The old man paused a bit hesitant to indulge the man any further. "His name?' he retorted. "His name's Marlon."

"Marlon...as in the Marlon Brando?"

"Yes! That's right...Brando. I loved him in that movie. What do you call that...that movie?"

"*Streetcar Named Desire*?" the officer blurted.

He smiled. "Yes! You're good. It's like you've read my mind."

"Stella! Stella!" The officer yelled out quietly as the waitress looked on and laugh.

"Great movie!" she blurted. "You know...that's my name!" She pointed at her name tag.

The officer laughed. "How about that?"

"Elijah, meet Stella." The officer grinned.

The old man couldn't withhold the silly exchange and smirked politely. "Great movie," he replied.

Without hesitation, the officer asked, "Been a while, huh?"

Eli gave him a serious look and pondered. "It has."

"Anyway, how is the soup?"

"It's good. Why don't you try yours?" The old man pointed to the bowl sitting in front of him.

"You know what, you look hungrier than me,' he said, pushing the bowl to the old woman. "Here."

"Thank you, but you ordered that for yourself, sir."

"No, it's okay. I had a good bit earlier. Please, take mine. I'd like to put it to good use, and you'll only get to taste this once. Might as well take the second. This will keep you warm. And…by the time you're done with the second bowl, you'll leave all your worries here."

"Well, thank you. That's awfully kind of you, sir."

The waitress stood idly by as she finished wiping the rest of the countertop while the men finish their late supper. "Is there anything else that I can get you?" she asked the old man.

"The soup tastes great! I would like to have some more, but I'm afraid that I'm filled," he replied. "I would love to come back and have some of your special soup again…if time permits."

"Well, that is kind of you, sir. Thank you," she replied as the officer left a twenty-dollar bill on the counter next to his glass of water.

"Can I get you something to take with you?" she asked the officer.

Glancing over to the old man, he said, "You've been more than accommodating. I thank you for your patience." His smile curled. "I just wanted to show my friend here that taking the time to taste God's great invention can be satisfying."

Without hesitation, Elijah interjected, "Ya know, my wife…she was a great cook."

"Is that so?" the officer replied.

"Yes, indeed she was. She used to cook for a rich family down in Georgia. She was a helper, a maid, ya know! She was great at it, and she was a gifted cook," he said proudly.

"Sounds like she can really cook, Eli." The officer turned as he folded his white napkin by the side of the glass.

"We were in love. She was quite a gal." His eyes sparkled.

"Where is she now?" the waitress asked with a candid stare.

"Oh…well she…she," he paused for a moment then resumed sipping his soup.

"Well?" The waitress insisted.

Eli hesitated, his face grew somber. "She passed away several years ago."

"I'm really sorry for your loss," the officer calmly asked. "I'm pretty sure that she's in a better place."

"I hope so. I pray that she's there when I go see her…one of these days."

"You will." The officer chuckled. "But for now, you've got to enjoy that soup…it's getting cold."

"She was quite a gal," he whispered as he reminisced. "We were married for almost forty years, and I was a lucky man. She and I were so in love, and she turned me into a better man. Because of her, I found my purpose. She kept me even-keeled and grounded."

"Purpose?" the officer asked. "Must be some calling."

"It was. My purpose was…to love her."

"That's quite a purpose…endearing one. Definitely a high calling."

"She was quite an amazing woman. Everyone she knew loved her. And everyone who knew her loved her. She carried herself with such grace. There was an aura about her, and I was the lucky man who came home to her."

"Quite a lady you got there, Eli," he replied.

The old man nodded and smiled. "She gave me two good young boys, Charles and Marlon."

"You told me that Marlon is in the military, but what about Charles? Where's he?"

"Charles is a pastor of a large church in Texas. He's made quite a name for himself. He's a great pastor with a large church. You see, he always been a very gifted speaker, and he possessed such intellect. He knows the Bible like the back of his hand."

"You must be very proud, Eli. Wow! Two sons: a pastor and a Green Beret. Quite a family you got there. Must be fun during the holidays," the officer gleefully replied.

Eli gave a blank stare, unable to reply to the officer's assumption.

Sam leaned closer. "Do you see them much?"

"I lived with Charles and his wife for quite some time. Marlon, I don't see him very often. Charles thought that it would be wise for me to see his brother since I haven't seen him and his family for quite some time."

"Well, the holidays are just around the corner. It must be good to see your boy when he returns from his deployment. Does he live in North Carolina?"

"I don't remember. My ticket says Atlanta, but I think he lives in North Carolina. Or...was it South Carolina?"

"So...you're not sure where he lives?" the officer asked.

"I can't remember. I'm supposed to meet him at a station. Charles told me that he'll be picking me up at the terminal."

"So, if Charles told you and you have a ticket heading to Atlanta, then he should be waiting for you...isn't he?"

"I'm sure he's waiting for me at the station. My son...he's very astute. He'll be there to meet me. Charles said so."

"You don't know, do you?"

The old man shook his head. "I'm not sure. To be honest with you. But I know that he'll be there to pick me up."

"Do you have his phone number? Maybe we can call him from the phone here."

"I...I...I had his phone number, but I can't find it."

"Maybe it's in your wallet."

"No, I checked. It's not there."

"Okay, well, why don't you tell me Charles's phone number so we can call him and ask for Marlon's phone number?"

"I don't have that either. You see, Charles placed all the phone numbers on my cell phone...and honestly, I can't find it."

"Hmm, well, I think that the best way for you to do to find your other son is to get to your intended destination first thing in the morning. I know for sure that a Green Beret would never leave his man behind. I'm sure he's waiting for you, and he'll be there when you get there."

Eli made an unassuming stare, slightly confused.

"Looks like you're done with those bowls. How was it?"

"Good. Very good. Thank you for the wonderful treat."

"Let's head on and head to the hotel. I'm pretty sure that you must be very tired from the trip."

The two men drove back to the hotel. Eli noticed a photo plastered under the visor over the officer's head.

"Is that your little girl?"

"Oh, that's my niece, Ally."

"Do you have any children?"

"I do."

"Where are they now?"

"He's still too young to remember me. I'm glad I still get to see them grow. My wife, well…she is a very strong woman and a good mother. I'm proud of her. It's a refreshing feeling, seeing your child grow right before you." He paused, fielding a blank stare. Then he smiled. "You see, Eli, children are like a garden. You tend to it, pay attention to it, till it, water it, fertilize it, open it for the sun and a lot of love…and they bloom on their own. If you plant them on bitter, hard soil, they will struggle. If you plant them on the rocks, they will struggle. But if you plant them on the right soil under the right sun, you will see them bloom in due season."

"I did what I could with what I had to raise my children the way my father raised me."

"Oh? And how's that?"

"Well, they are good boys. I was…well, I was a bit easy on the older one. He was a good kid. But the younger one…well, he was a bullheaded, strong-willed child that wanted his way."

The younger one…you mean Marlon?

Eli nodded.

"Charles was easy, we were fortunate to have him. See, my wife and I…well, we tried for so long to have our own child. But it wasn't easy, ya know. See, Charles was not our first. Two years after we were married, she got pregnant. It came as a surprise to me. After all, we were not trying. I grew anxious after she told me that she was pregnant. We just didn't have the means, and I wasn't ready. I felt like we were not ready. But she was happy. And four weeks after she told me, after she came home from a long day's work and…' He paused. 'I will never forget that day. See, maybe it was me who caused this…for not wanting the child, or maybe she overworked herself. But somehow, God was…well, he took the baby away. That night, she came home exhausted and stressed. She was cooking a meal when she began having some sharp pains on her tummy, and she began to panic. She noticed that it was the baby, and by the time we got to the hospital, we have already lost him."

"I'm saddened by your loss. It must have been traumatic having to lose a child. Did you ever get over that pain?"

Eli nodded. "I don't think you'll ever forget it. You move on, but you could never forget losing someone before they were born. Never have I ever loved some one as deeply, one I've never met. I passed through the deepest sadness. These dark days were long and empty, and the whiskey... it numbed the pain. I drank until I could no longer feel anything except... nothing. But my wife, she held on. She stood strong, every day, by my side. She kept me sane, and it was her that made me realize that I could do better. She didn't give up, but she needed me in the present. So I fought on. We grieved for many, many years."

"And when our eyes ran dry and our hearts beat again, we chose to move on and try again. After I found a job at the school, we decided to try having a child. But it was more difficult. Getting pregnant became a chore, and she could not get pregnant, no matter how we tried, and the doctors couldn't give us a reason why. It placed a lot of pressure on our marriage, and we grew despondent over the years. All those years spent on prayers took its toll. It broke my heart to see my wife struggle through the pain of being, unable to bear a child. She grew sad over time when she watched the children she babysat grew up in front of her when she couldn't have her own." He hung his head shamefully.

"It devastated her. And I felt powerless. For me, I began to doubt God. I grew angry, and we began to resent each other. But we never gave up hope, and we continued to serve in our church, hoping that someday, God will hear our prayers and grant us a child.' His eyes glistened under weigh of memories. 'Some years later, for some unknown reason, she got pregnant. We'd given up hoping that our prayers were going to be answered. Funny how God answers prayers!' He smiled. "'When we finally let go, our prayers were answered."

"That's quite a miracle, Eli."

"Ya know, before she told me that she was pregnant, she still doubted herself. It took her several weeks to wrap her head around it...that she was going to have a baby. I've never seen such happiness, such joy. Can't forget that glow on her face. She wore that face for nine straight months."

"You know Eli...I appreciate your openness, but I just have to ask. What about Marlon?"

"Marlon? Well, after, we wanted to get our lives in order. It was finally time for us to buy our dream home. We couldn't imagine having a child so soon. We wanted to spend all our time and energy with our son, and we relished the days when we could be a family. We were not planning to have another child, at least not until we knew that we could afford to have another one. It was difficult enough to raise a child and having to work at the same time to make ends meet, but having another one? We just didn't want it. At least not until Charles was old enough to feed himself."

"So, Marlon came along without being invited, huh?"

"Marlon wasn't planned. It took us many years to have a child. We were certain that it would take us another five years to have another. So, we got careless."

"Careless?" The officer chuckled.

"Best way to put it…we weren't expecting to be expecting so soon," He paused briefly. The car pulled off to the side of the road and parked in front of the hotel.

Eli opened the door of car. "I really appreciate your kindness, sir."

"Wait! Hold on, you were telling me about Marlon. You can't just leave in the middle of the story. You have to finish what you started. Tell me," the officer asserted as Eli paused and shut the door and sat back down.

"Well, what else do you want to know?"

"Marlon…you never told me anything good about Marlon."

"Well, Marlon was a strong-willed child, energetic, and stubborn to a fault, yet confident. He was also very assertive. That boy never relented until he got his way. He was always like this since the day he was born. Now, Charles, on the other hand, was very smart, perceptive, kind, and full of life. Charles was a great kid."

"I'm pretty sure Marlon is who he is because of what he was. Your past can't be too far away from the present…at least not in this lifetime."

"You know, Marlon is a good kid. He's just…' He tilted his head in shame. 'Different."

"All kids are different. Some just require more attention."

"I don't know about Marlon though. I just can't plant a finger on it. He's a good kid, but he always challenged me, tried my patience up to no end. I was a bit harder on the boy."

"Expectation, is the worst man-made invention."

Eli was confused by his remark. "I guess. We do expect a lot of ourselves."

The officer turned off the ignition. "I think you may have made a breakthrough here."

The old man looked over. His eyes were hazy. A teardrop rolled down his face.

"You were hard on the kid, but the kid turned out alright. But what I'd like to know is have you ever told him that you were proud of him?" He paused and waited for a quick response. But the old man remained silent. "Have you ever told him that? Or have you ever told him that you love him?" he whispered.

The old man shrugged off the man's intrusive question.

"Well?"

Eli grew petulant. "Well what? I've told you everything. What else do you want? A sincere apology? A long confession?' He paused as the man withdrew. 'That's easy for you to say. You didn't raise the boy."

"You're right. I didn't, but God gave you that boy. Don't you think that he deserves a reply?"

"So, you God now?" he replied sarcastically, growing agitated for such intrusive question.

"Tell you what, let's just leave it just the way it is. You're right. He's your son.

Forgive me for intruding. I just want to ask you the important questions, something that carries a meaning. Sooner or later, you'll be given the opportunity to do as I have asked. Sooner or later, your son will ask you the same question. I just want to let you know that it doesn't matter what you think or feel. What matters is how you say it that will carry through a lifetime. If you love your son, then tell him. If you are proud of him, then tell him. It doesn't take much, but it means more than anything you could give. If you can give something, it's the love that could never be washed away. It's the act that won't be forgotten, it's the words that will never fade, and it's the faith that brings it all together. Grace doesn't end in us saying that we are loved and forgiven. Grace never stops for one man's doubts. Its' what allows us to see through God's eyes. If you love your son, it's not because he earned it, not because he deserved it, but because he's a gift."

The officer paused and turned on the ignition. "Thank you for your honestly, Eli. It was great to have talked to you. Sooner or later, we will meet once again. Hopefully, you'll be ready to answer the tough questions."

The old man opened the door without saying a word. He offered a handshake as a gesture of gratitude. He simply looked at him with a genteel smile and nodded.

"Hey! Tell your son he's a hero in my book," he hollered as the old man proceeded to enter the hotel.

That night, the old man could not earn a moment of sleep. He struggled to keep his eyes closed. He was restless but groggy at the same time, hoping to steal some rest. But their profound discourse bothered him, leaving him to ponder on every word that surfaced from the crevices of his soul. The officer's query was intrusive and direct. But it was poignant, aimed straight through the heart. He understood the emotional struggles, the regrets, and the heartache, as if he saw right through him.

He never encountered anyone as wise—at least not since his wife passed away. Their meeting appeared serendipitous rather than coincidental. The man offered no hint of threat or ill motive, but inviting in every way. Eli sensed a blissful peace with his presence; a distinct spiritual manifestation that he felt as he stood by his wife's bedside that moment she drew her last breath. An overwhelming love that emanated from God's presence on the day he got saved.

Throughout the night, he sifted through the broken past with jumbled pieces that felt surreal; both the good and bad were entwined within a short lifetime. He reminisced on a few blissful moments and ignored the painful ones. He vividly recalled that day when he ran into a pulchritudinous young woman at a feed store, and the world that appeared dull, cold and fast began to thaw from that moment when he found a reason to strive. She appeared without any warning on that fateful day, the memory was so vivid that he could smell the distinct fragrance of her perfume. That day was seared through his eyes, a day like no other when she walked through the door. It was a time of his prime; he was young, confident, and brash.

It was during a sunny Saturday afternoon when he was told to run by the feed store to purchase a bag of wheat for his boss. Since no one was eager to go, he gladly volunteered to run the errand, perhaps to break the monotony of the day. As he came to the doorstep, we has distracted by a blaring car horn as it zoomed through the street. He was startled to see the car racing in the middle of the street, carving its tires on the dirt road. Not far behind was the sheriff in hot pursuit. "*Whoo! That was close! He drew a brief sigh of relief. Ain't no faster than me. I would be long gone if I was driving that car!*"

Chapter Seven

"This is annoying!" He thought as he drove through the empty road. The trip seemed to have taken longer than expected. His truck seated only two to three passengers, and the vehicle offered little comfort for prolonged travel. *"Quite a trek! I haven't seen this much action since Wanat. It felt good, really good. I think I'm ready. Darak can say whatever he wants, but I'm ready to redeploy and be with my men."*

He pulled up his sleeve over his neck and glanced over his army-issued wristwatch. Its dial tucked under his wrist to conceal its glare. He squinted down, rubbing his yes to see the time as dawn ascended. He glanced around to see if there were any cars parked nearby, and any sign of people could mean that a new train might be arriving. After a few minutes, no one came. He leaned back on the seat and pulled his collars over his shoulders and retired to earn some sleep. He was tired and groggy, but he couldn't earn any lengthy sleep. He looked on his right side and noticed the prescription bottle lying down. He opened it and swallowed a couple of pills then chugged it down with water. He glanced around again to see if anyone had arrived. Once again, all he noticed was the lady tending the ticket booth fidgeting with her nails, waiting for passengers to arrive. After several minutes of waiting, he slowly dozed off.

"Action left!" one of the men yelled out. "Action left!"

He let go of Robben, and when he came to his senses, he carefully mounted his Kevlar over his head. The men appeared calm as they await the status of the two men who were inside the house. The house was flattened by the enormous explosion. Marlon stood up and returned to the Humvee. Slightly disoriented, he slowly radioed back for medical evacuation of the wounded.

Without any warning, several gunshots from the mountain ridge to the west zinged past him. The men sprung into defensive position and returned fire at the enemy. One of the men behind him, a highly skilled army sniper, was picking off the enemy from the hilltop. As he reloaded his weapon, a bullet pierced through his neck, instantly knocking him to the ground. He tried getting up, and as he bent down to reload, he fell again and died. As the medic tried to apply first aid, but several bullets riddled through his torso, his thigh, and his stomach and killed him instantly.

Marlon and the rest of the team noticed this, and fear engulfed them. Marlon was taken aback, still recovering from a state of shock. The blast caused severe ringing in his ears and the headache quickly worsened. Then he stood up and kept his wits, completely exposing himself to the enemy fire, but he needed to do this for his men, to show that he was still in command. He collected his thoughts hoping to center his bearing. He pointed at Framm.

"Framm! Get those men and set up a DP! Do it now!"

"Sir! We're surrounded. We can't possibly deploy a defensive perimeter. We need to exfil! Sir!" Framm responded angrily.

"Do it, Sergeant. That's an order! Do it!" he yelled out as he cocked his rifle. The enemy firing the left side of the column was relentless. Bullets from the enemy's Kalashnikov's whizzed by them and hit one of his men on the thigh. He took the man and dragged him on the other side of the Humvee where they hunkered for cover.

"Get some men to man that duce. Pin them down…suppressive fire!' he yelled out to Framm. 'And get me a medic here, asap."

"Sir. We can't stay here. We have to start moving!" Framm contested while the rest of the men engaged the enemy, firing at the direction of the incoming enemy fire.

"We're not going to leave Miller and Khal no matter what!"

"Sir, if we stay, we'll lose more men!"

"No, Sergeant, we will not leave the first sergeant and Khal. Get those men to save ammo. Do not engage in the open." He looked at the clay house where the meeting took place; it was obliterated, all that remained was a heap of rubble. Body parts were scattered in close proximity.

"Sir! The first sergeant is gone. You must order a retreat!"

"Noted, Sergeant! Get me my damn medic. I need him here now!" He walked briskly over to the next vehicle and grabbed the HCLOS radio.

"Break! Break! Echo Two-Four, come in. Echo Two-Four, come in. This is Whiskey Five-Six, over."

He waited frantically for a prompt reply. "Whiskey Five-Six, this is Echo Two-Four." the man from the base responded, his voice was drowned under the static.

"Be advised, team is under enemy attack! I repeat, my team is under enemy attack, over."

"Whiskey Five-Six, do you need immediate reinforcements? Over."

He thought for a few seconds, pondering the current situation slowly slipping out of control. "Negative, Echo. Situ under control."

"Copy that, no reinforcements required, over."

"Situ under control. Need immediate Medivac. Four K-I-A. Two mortal, Over."

"Roger that. Medivac relay in twenty mikes, over."

Framm approached him by the side of the road behind the second Humvee while firing his rifle at the hilltop.

"Echo Two-Four, be advised. We are under enemy attack. Small arms fire and RPGs, requesting for immediate artillery support. We are under attack!" he screamed.

"What is your coordinates Whiskey Five-Six."

"Unit intact. Critical injuries. Still combat effective."

"Enemy location?"

"Danger close, enemy within range. Whiskey Five-Six, out." He ends the call and dials in for artillery support. "Big Stick, this is Whiskey Five-Six, team leader requesting fire mission. Big Stick, this is Whiskey Five-Six, team leader requesting fire mission."

The radio crackled, "This is Big Stick, what's the coordinates?"

"Grid Tango Alpha 5-5-7-8-4-1. Direction 3400, range from point 1, 1800. Left 2200, drop 400, distance 2655. Two to four hundred hostiles entrenched uphill. "Fire for effect, over. Keep it coming." Marlon calmly added.

"Fire for effect, roger. Grid Tango Alpha 5-5-7-8-4-1 Grid Tango Alpha 5-5-7-8-4-1. Direction 3400, range from point 1, 1800. Left 2200, drop 400, distance 2655. Incoming in Tree-Mike."

Marlon looked at the rest of the men around him. "Artillery incoming in Tree-mikes. Tell the men to save ammo until air support arrives."

In a little over three minutes, the cannons began firing. Each deafening explosion landed with precision on top of the enemy hunkered down on the hilltop. After several minutes of intense bombardment, the attackers ceased firing at Marlon and his team.

He threw the HCLOS radio on to the seat, and Framm stood right next to him.

"What is it, Sergeant?"

"Sir, haji is concentrating their assault on the middle of our group. They're closing in. Gunshots will intensify. They won't stop. Looks like haji has doubled in strength."

He yells at Framm. "Keep that perimeter tight, Sergeant. Get Miller out of there!"

"Sir, are you sure about this?"

"We don't have a choice. If we retreat, they will be posting Miller's mangled body online. We have to get him out of there and take him home. That's an order."

"The injured men, sir?"

"Take them to the nearest house and tend to the men. We will have to hold until reinforcements arrive. Make sure that the perimeters are set."

Without warning, a second mortar shell exploded nearby several soldiers who were firing against the enemy. The explosion was at close proximity, several feet behind them. The shrapnel zipped through over their heads while few went straight to their vests. Luckily, the four men were not seriously injured from the explosion. But the impact of the explosions inflicted serious concussions that left several men unconscious. After a few seconds, they regained their senses, then quickly hunkered down for cover. Their ears bled as they called out for medical attention. Marlon ordered his men to move and find cover behind the nearby houses until they were able to regroup, gather their wounded, and make a hasty retreat when the gunship arrives.

Chapter Eight

The crisp, cool morning felt surreal; too much had happened within the past twenty-four hours, peeling himself out of his element. The errand was growing burdensome and annoying. The wait and the travel, along with the pills, left him groggy through the night. For several hours, he dozed on and off inside the pickup, gaining some semblance of sleep-a pleasant reprieve from the unwanted errand. He waited until the station opened for the day. As the six o'clock sunrise descended with the Southern heat, he felt the cold chill dissipate, but he remained languorous-loafing under the serene morning. That peaceful moment was what he needed as he waited in quiet cogitation only to be awakened by the blistering sound of screeching tires entering the parking lot. When he turned, he noticed a rusty white Cuprice abruptly stopping to park at the handicap zone. He did not expect to see an old lady emerging out of the car. She hastily ran toward the terminal, then she opened the ticket booth inside; she was the only attendant present inside the terminal. Marlon couldn't believe seeing an old lady, petite and frail, running so quickly to attend an empty booth. *"Wow, I could really use a soldier like her."* He smiled. He waited until she was settled and proceeded to inquire her for further information.

He sat up and noticed his shirt soaked in sweat. Then he got out of the truck and approached the old lady waiting begrudgingly inside the five-by-six ticket booth. Her thick silver stringy hair tied on a ponytail rested loosely over her left shoulder—a tight weave that appeared out of place. He trotted up to the thick, glass pane and nodded at the old lady.

"Good morning to you!" she replied with a condescending tone, slightly annoyed.

"How can I help?" She grinned.

"Good morning ma'am! Um…I'm not here to buy a ticket, but I was wondering if you could help me. When will the next train arrive?" he asked.

"It should be within the hour." She paused and looked at the clock and the arrival schedule on the black canvas hanging behind her. "Yes, it should be within the hour." She glanced over to him with sardonic face as she tinkered with her silver bracelet.

"I'm looking for my father. He's was supposed to arrive here last night, and I haven't yet seen him. He's about five-foot ten, old black guy." But the old lady replied with a disdainful look in her face. "Is that how you always end a conversation?" She asked. Marlon closed his eyes in disbelief.

"Well, do you know what he looks like? Maybe I can try and help."

"Honestly, I actually cannot really describe how he looks like. See, it's been years since the last time I saw him. He's sporting a short beard… sorta goatee. He should be grayed, his eyes…well, they're slightly slanted. He looks like a serious man who could be easily mistaken as someone angry." He added. His face appeared slightly dumbfounded; his eyebrows furrowed, his eyes squinted.

"Well, would you happen to have a photo?" she asked, "After all, he is your father…isn't he?" she added, slightly curious.

"Umm…I wish I did," he replied, "Well, how 'bout this…did you see an angry black man arrive here last night?"

She smiled with one raised brow. "Angry black man? What'd you mean by that?" she asked a petulant stare. "It's none o' my business, but was your father always an angry person?"

"Oh no, he just always looks angry," he replied, eager to end the conversation.

"I'm not sure what you mean young man. But to answer your question…I left work after three o'clock yesterday afternoon, and I have not seen any old, angry African American all day yesterday. I've seen several colored men leave the station, but none matched the description you made."

Marlon sensed her petulance. "Colored? Okay, that's fine. Sorry for the trouble. Thank you." He began to walk away then turned. "Oh, if I may, I came across an older man last night. He was cleaning the platform at the back of the station. Would you happen to know him? Maybe he can give me some info."

"An older gentleman?" she asked, slightly perplexed. Her face grew suspicious. "Yes, he…he was sweeping the floor, and I asked him a question, but he just disappeared. I wonder if he's around. Maybe I can talk to him."

"Sir, there ain't nobody here working at night…At least not that I know of. No one here comes at night to clean the entire station since Ol' man Jacob passed away five years ago. The young janitor who cleans the station arrives at noon and leaves before three. And if that's who you are referring to, he happens to be a nice young black man. He should be here by noon."

Marlon was taken aback, clearly confused. "This is a joke, right?" he asked with an incredulous smile.

"If you are making it up, yes! It sounds crazy, and it's much too early for that.' she answered. 'Are you okay?"

"Yes, yes.' He paused. 'You know what, thank you. That's all I need. You sure you're right? That you haven't seen an older black man arrive here?"

"Young man, I would love to help you, but if you can't give me a full description, a picture of some sort that I may recognize him, then I'm afraid that I can't. Now, if you would excuse me, I need to assist the gentleman who is waiting behind you." She waives him off.

"Thank you." He walked away. *"This is a stupid joke,"* he thought. *"How can I find him if no one is willing to help?"* He walked back to his truck, annoyed and slightly dumbfounded of the woman's reply. *"She's probably too old to know anyways. That old man was real, I know it. She just couldn't remember. But if she's delirious, what does that make me? If that old man did not exist, which he did, then who was he? Why was he asking me questions rather than answer mine?"*

He walked back slowly to his truck and waited for the train to arrive. He realized that he had not eaten for the past twelve hours. His body had been subjected to countless days skipping meals on patrols during his combat tour. He had grown privy to the laborious days waiting, hiking and carrying heavy weight on rocky mountainous cliff with little food or water to drink, and this endeavor was common-except that the mission was insignificant. He grew pensive and decided to head out to the nearest fast food restaurant to grab a small meal to get him through the day. He pulled up his cell phone and searched for his brother's phone number when he stumbled upon one of his men's phone number.

"Robben, I haven't seen this phone number for quite some time. He mentioned to me that he grew in this city." He pressed the green button to call. The outbound call seemed fleeting, the young man was really dead, but he needed to check if the number existed. He was surprised to hear when the phone rang on the other end. *"Well, I hope no one answers. Wouldn't know what to say. But it's worth try. Maybe I can finally put this kid to rest."* After ringing several times, the voicemail came on.

"Hello, this is the Robben's residence, we are not here to answer the phone, but if you leave your name, message, and phone number, we will get back to you as soon as possible. Thank you and enjoy your day." The recorded greeting ended with a beep.

"Umm, hi! I was calling for Mr. Robben, Gracen's father? You may not know me or heard of me, but I was in town for a couple of hours, and I wanted to call to talk to you about your son. My name is…Captain Coe, Marlon Coe. Please call me at your convenience at 9-0-8-6-1-2-7-7-1-5. If you wish to talk, I will be at a train station at eleven hundred hours. Thank you." He ended the call, hoping not to hear a response after he had left town. But deep down, he knew that he needed to see Grayson's parents to bring closure to their son's unfortunate death. He placed the phone down without making any further calls to his brother. Perhaps until he had eaten his breakfast.

He found a small diner next to a gas station. He gassed up then parked at the diner. There was no drive through, so he had to park, sit, and order a meal until it was time to leave. When he entered, he noticed some men sitting by the booth, all four of them sipping their morning coffee. They appeared haggard from a prolonged travel. He also noticed several police officers sitting by the other end of the corner of the diner, gorging on their breakfast, to beat the morning rush and start their shift. No one seemed to mind his entrance.

It was a cold reception; no one bothered to stand up and salute the man who entered the room. He was accustomed to men waiting on him, standing in attention upon his entrance, greeting or saluting him by the doorway. On this morning, no one seemed to care. He looked at every customer sitting down, but no one reciprocated and nodded to greet him. He decided to sit by the bar where it was vacant; no one bothered to sit across the bar. Everyone was caught up with their own agenda, mingling among themselves on the day's routine. He sat down and picked up a small folded menu. The waitress approached, but she appeared tired. She poured the coffee into his cup without uttering a single word. She was completely oblivious to the lonely visitor sitting at the booth.

He glanced around to see if anyone bothered to look and check on him, but no one paid attention. They were caught up quietly scarfing through their morning breakfast. He could hear the noises on the background- the silverware clanked off the porcelain cups, and people sniffling and fending off the cold. The officers barely parsed any words to each other, and the truckers could not speak past their grunting.

The whole scene was reminiscent of the past when he and his men sat inside the barracks, waiting for orders to arrive, trying to pass time with silence and reflection. The quietness seemed familiar; it spurred indelible memories of tremendous angst where a sudden enemy attack could alter the course of their lives. But the scene brought a sense of longing, a fleeting, sinking feeling of insignificance. No one knew him nor hinted any interest. He was surrounded by strangers in a familiar place; a place where people came to eat and mingle, parsing words to pass off time and fill their appetite. He looked at the menu, but his mind wondered into the past.

"So what will it be?" the waitress asked.

He gave no response. He was caught in a deep thought, his eyes fixed on the menu, and his face fielded a blank stare.

She leaned closer. "Hun! Are you going to order? Or are you going to keep staring at that menu?" she whispered.

Marlon's eyes twitched as came to his senses. "Oh! I'll have the regular," he answered as he folded the menu down to the side.

"Regular? I just gave you the regular coffee. Want to be more spontaneous?" she cracked a smile.

He looked up, sensing the thick sarcasm on her voice. "It's been a while," he mumbled.

"Okay…do you want more time?"

"Um…no, no. Let's umm…let's start with some eggs." He replied in a jovial tone in reply to ease her assertion.

"Scrambled? Or sunny side up?"

"Scrambled."

"Eggs? That's it? You look like you could use some more there, mister."
He looked around to see what the other men had on their plates. "I'll um…I'll have some sausage too, and grits, two of each," he smiled politely.

As he sipped his coffee, he overheard the police officers mingling more distinctly, discussing their past and recent encounters while on duty. The conversation turned loud as the men joked about the people they recently encountered and apprehended. Marlon couldn't resist and began to listen closely. Their overt and condescending tone involving a person's unfortunate mishaps bothered him, and his stomach began to churn, almost to the point of vomiting—leaving a bad taste in his mouth. His recent heroic encounter with the injured policeman felt seemingly pedestrian. *"These guys are scumbags. Puts a whole new twist on protect and serve."* He could also hear the truck drivers constantly grunting at each other's comments. They hardly parsed any words, just simple nods and short, jumbled syllables to get through the meal. The men seemed content and exhausted from prolonged driving. As he waited for his meal, he heard one of the truckers mumble with a strong Southern twang; his old baseball cap was stained sweat that hung unevenly on his shaggy hair.

"Crazy weather out there!" the men said.

"It's not the weather, it's the other driver that's slowing us down," an old man replied.

"Don't care about the weather. The gas, that's the source of the problem! Each time I run a route, it's costing me a few more dollars out of my own hard earned money. I ain't getting no help from my boss. Not from no one!" he scoffed.

Marlon smirked after hearing this. *"You guys should seriously get a life and get over yourselves. You think you're life is hard? Try getting shot at by the Taliban. Or get your buddies blown off…or better yet, watch your friends die in front of you…seeing if you'd care about the traffic or the weather. Geez! I'm glad I didn't sign up to defend freedom. Glad I signed up to watch over my buds! These guys can't carry a good conversation in the middle of a good, hot meal."* He subtly shook his head. After several minutes, his meal arrived. The waitress winked at him for waiting.

"Hun, you are one patient man. Thanks for waiting. Coffee's in the house!" she winked.

Marlon cracked a big smile. "Thank you. Good coffee!"

The officers took a quick glance at him, slightly curious. One of the men facing him nodded at Marlon as he made a quick glance once again. He appeared perturbed that the man sitting at next to the counter who seemed interested and curious. He kept staring at Marlon. Marlon felt he was being watch under suspicion. As he went on eating his meal, one of the officers decided to strike up a conversation out of curiosity.

"How's the coffee?" he blurted loudly.

Marlon simply ignored the fleeting gesture.

"You gonna let me repeat myself?" he waited for an answer.

Marlon looked over his shoulders and noticed the officer staring directly at him. The officer was an older man. His peppered gray hair revealed his long tenure serving in the force. His partner was a younger officer, no older than twenty-five. The booth was about ten feet away. Everyone heard the officer's question, but no one replied.

"You asking me?" Marlon replied nonchalantly.

"No! I'm asking the waitress! She obviously needs to tell me how the coffee tastes. Of course I'm asking you! I'm looking at you!"

Marlon grew indignant. "Good!" he replied.

"Good? What the…what kind of answer is that?"

"You asked me a question. I gave you an answer, Officer," Marlon quipped.

"You believe this guy?" He looked at the other man sitting in front. "Okay, I guess that's how you want to be treated—a stranger?" He laughed as he shook his head. "You from around here? Or is that good too?"

Marlon turned and looked defiantly at the officers sitting by the booth. "No. I'm not from around here."

"So, you're visiting?" the other officer asked firmly, a bit annoyed at Marlon's nonchalant demeanor.

"No, no…I uh…I drove here."

"Drove from where?"

"From Bragg, Fort Bragg." He sighed. "Home of the Green Beret. You heard of them."

"Is that so?" The young officer asked. "I know a very good friend who serves with the Rangers. Maybe you know him!"

"If you're asking me, I know a lot of Rangers. What's his name?"

"Spotswood, Andy."

"Andy Spotswood. No, sorry name doesn't sound familiar."

"You're with the Rangers, aren't you?"

"I was…for a time being, but I got bored and joined the Special Forces."

"And you don't know or heard of Spotswood?"

Marlon shook his head. "No, sorry. Am I supposed to?"

"You're telling me that you're special ops, and you haven't heard of Spotswood?"

"No, is he related to John Rambo? What unit is he in? Who's his CO?"

"CO?"

"Who's his commanding officer?" he replied with condescending tone.

"Don't know. He and I go way back from college. Actually, he and my older brother attended college together, and he…he and I met once."

"He was the reason why I joined the force."

"Were you former military?"

"No, no. I just joined the police to keep close to home…I guess."

"Huh! That's interesting." Marlon resumed eating his meal.

"Interesting?" The older officer blurted as he turned toward him. "You're saying he's not good enough? Is that it?"

"Yes! That's actually what I am saying." He smirked.

"Just because you're Special Forces doesn't make you better than him, son."

"Ah. Okay."

"Okay what?' the older officer interrupted. "Son, I've been with the force for thirty years, and the men and women I've met, the ones who served, don't carry an attitude like you. Some kinda hotshot!" the officer contend.

"I'm no special. It's just a name, Officer.' He turned and looked at him. 'It's just a label, that's all. We're good, but we're just people…like you. If I have offended you and your partner there…then I never meant to do so."

"You really are a difficult man to talk to. No wonder you're alone."

"Yup!" Marlon mumbled.

"Well, I was going to thank you and pay for your meal, but since you want to be a jerk, good luck!"

Marlon shook his head and smiled politely.

"Let's go," the officer said to his younger partner.

The two men walked out slowly, gazing at Marlon eating his meal, waiting for a quick reply or a quip to justify a reasonable arrest.

The three men sitting quietly on the next booth looked at him; one of them smiled at him.

As the officers stepped out, one of the truckers stood up and walked over to Marlon immediately. He reached down to his wallet and took out a twenty dollar bill and placed it on the counter.

"Thank you for your service." The man reached out and offered to shake his hand.

Marlon, a bit surprised, shook the man's hand. "Thank you, but you didn't have to do that."

"Oh, I insist." He paused briefly. "I've seen that tattoo," he said, pointing to his left arm.

Marlon looked down on his tattoo just below his left elbow. It was a dagger planted through the tip of the black skull.

Marlon was surprised to hear that someone knew of his unit's distinct tattoo. "You've seen this before?" he asked with a curios tone.

"Few are chosen to give all," the man replied.

Marlon was surprised to hear it. He blushed, but he was bewildered. "Who was your son?"

The man cleared his throat, he was a bit choked up, "Robben."

Marlon stood up and slowly raised his right arm and saluted him. His eyes narrowed, glistening with tears. "I wasn't expecting to see you, sir!" His eyes lit up.

"My wife told me that you left a message on our voicemail. I was on my way to Savannah, and I stopped by to grab a hearty breakfast before heading off." The man sat next to him as the other men proceeded and shook his hand upon their departure.

"Wow! This is quite a moment." Marlon grinned, delighted and anxious. His emotions mixed and his demeanor steadfast, anticipating to field questions regarding Robben's last days.

"I just want to say, thank you." The man paused as he pulled down his cap. "Captain Coe. I want to thank you for looking out for my son."

"You're son died honorably in the face of danger, fighting alongside the men he loved," Marlon replied softly.

"He was a good kid…a bit stubborn and rambunctious, but a good kid."

"He was a good man and a brave soldier. He gave his life for his country and his buddies.' He paused. 'Your son…he died in my arms. He was dead before the medic got there. It was sudden. It came so fast. We didn't have much time to react and save him.' He began to sob. 'I wish that I was the one who took that hit. I'm so sorry for your loss."

The old man patted him on the right shoulder and slowly embraced him. "You have no need to apologize. I want to thank you, not blame you. It was…it was just his time to go.' The man sobbed quietly. 'He would have preferred it this way. He was just a boy when he left, but he did what every able good man would have done, and he died as a man."

Marlon nodded. "You know, he was slotted for a two-week leave a week before the assault. He gave that slot to one of my buddies whose wife just had a new baby…their first one."

The old man began to sob. "That's just how he is…always looking out for his buddies. As the oldest of three, he always took care of his two young sisters. Always noble, headstrong, adventurous, and even-keeled. You know, he always talked about you, that he never liked going on patrol because you always had to stay at the front. But he loved that about you. He admired you greatly. I've prayed for him to find a mentor as he grew older. And I'm glad that he was assigned to your unit. He told me once that you were the consummate professional,' he said with a pensive stare. 'I want to thank you for taking care of your men as a good, honorable soldier."

Marlon grabbed the man's right arm and whispered, "If there's anything that I can do…anything at all to appease your loss…please, tell me," he said with deep conviction.

"You have done more than I could have asked for. My son…It was just his time. No matter how hard I hold on to him, it would not have changed anything. I'd give anything to trade places with him. We serve a purpose in this life and the next. When that is finished, we have lived the life that Almighty God called us to do. One way or the other, there is a meaning involved in our decisions. It is the substance that is important when we serve our purpose. What matters is that we find our calling, serve our purpose, and go home. My son found life serving alongside his brothers. I am deeply grateful for his sacrifice, and the country is indebted for it. My wife and I are deeply saddened and heartbroken for his death. But we grieved, we healed and cherish the memories to find peace, and we move on.' He paused briefly. 'Do what my boy would have wanted you to do. Get moving and don't look back." The man stood up and left a billfold on the counter. "There's no need to apologize." He nodded and embraced him.

"Thank you for your sacrifice. Maybe now I can earn a slight semblance of peace for his passing." Marlon held on tightly, his eyes glistened.

The man wrote down a phone number on a napkin, folded it, and handed it over to him. "I want you to know that you can call me anytime you want to, and my wife and I would enjoy your company if whenever you have the chance to visit this town once again. She would love to talk to you about Gracen and she would love to hear more about you and your team. If you ever need a place to call home, you have my number."

They shook hands and bid farewell. The man walked out and joined his friends waiting outside. Marlon stood in awe, quite mesmerized by the event that unfolded.

"This can't be a coincidence. No one shows up in a diner, and…wow! This is quite a day." He took a sip of coffee and left some money for the tip.

"Hey, hun!" the waitress said as she wiped the counter. "Thank you for your service!"

As he walked into his car, he noticed one of the officers writing a citation in the front of his vehicle. He was indignant. "Excuse me! Is there a problem, Officer?"

"Nope, no problem with your parking," the older officer replied. His partner remained seated inside the patrol car. 'There's mud on your tag."

"Then can I help you?" Marlon approached him.

The officer ripped the ticket citation off the pad and slapped the white copy on his chest. "Yes, as a matter of fact, you can.' He grinned. 'You can pay for the ticket when you appear in court. You're tag has also expired."

Marlon replied with an angry stare, his eyebrows furrowed. "Thank you for your service!" he asserted with sarcasm.

"You got a problem, son?" the officer stared at him and approached him, standing squarely close to him and slaps the ticket to his chest.

Marlon smirked. "I guess not. I mean, I deserved the ticket. After all, I served my country to protect men like you. So there's no problem. I'll pay for the stupid ticket."

"Listen, I will only say this once.' The old man pointed his finger at his face. 'If you have a problem with me, you can come with me to the station. We have a warm cell saved up for lawbreakers like you. My partner and I would love to take you there with or without an invitation. So, you have two choices: you can stand there and get cuffed, or you can get to your truck and scram, boy!"

Marlon grabbed the ticket and walked to his truck. Then he turned around as he opened the door, his lips pursed. "I already got ticketed for this yesterday. Oh, and by the way, you're welcome. I guess this is the thanks that I get for saving guys like you." He entered his trucked and drove off.

The officer shook his head got into his patrol car, his partner stood outside, anxious and nervous, waiting to depart. Without hesitation, the patrol car followed him as he drove off and headed back to the station.

After several miles, he noticed that he had several messages on his voicemail. He forgot and left his cell phone in the truck earlier. He opened it and played the messages.

"Marlon, this is Charles. I got your message. What do you mean Dad wasn't there? Call me as soon as you get this!"

He deleted it and moved on to the next message. "Marlon! Charles. Where are you? Why can't you return my call? Pick up your phone and call."

Marlon was agitated after hearing this. Again, he deleted the second message. Still, two more messages remained to be heard.

"Marlon, this is Cheryl. I have not heard a reply from you. Please call me. It's about your daughters upcoming birthday. I need to know if you are coming to visit. She's…she's been asking for you every day. She's eager to know if you are coming. Any reply would be nice. Bye!"

He briefly pondered on the message and moved on the fourth one. "Marlon, this is Colonel Darak. I need you to call me. It's about the upcoming trial. Call me as soon as possible."

"What is going on? I'm gone for an hour, and I get four new messages?' he thought. *'Why can't they call me when I'm available?"* He glanced at the rearview mirror and noticed the patrol car tagging closely.

He arrived at the train station just when the first train made its way to the terminus. Only a handful of people came in waiting to fetch their guests. After he parked, he noticed the patrol car had parked by the entrance. The officers had stalked him, waiting and anticipating for him to make the wrong move, their eyes gazing on him with contempt. They were bent on arresting him. He calmly walked over to the entrance and gave them a stern look as he passed by taunting them utter defiance. He proceeded to wait by the platform keenly aware of their presence nearby. He anticipated this move. He expected them to follow suit. The two men poked around; each one from the opposite end of the terminus slowly approached him, hoping to find a reasonable cause to arrest him.

As the train arrived, only a few passengers disembarked and greeted their loved ones. Nothing out of the ordinary occurred. No one who appeared from the train closely resembled his father. As he waited, no one else exited the train, then he noticed that the officers stood squarely by him. "You're waiting for someone?" the officer asked.

"Yes, as a matter of fact, I was. Why'd you followed me here, Officer?" he asked as he grew more agitated.

"You've heard of probable cause, right?" the officer replied, hinting some aggression.

"And your cause is?" Marlon shook his head.

"I think you're bad news. It's written all over your face."

"Do you see me carrying a weapon, Officer?' he replied, 'Do you notice anything suspicious…aside from my license plates?"

The young officer inched his way behind him. Then the two men closed in. Sensing that he was about to be arrested, Marlon perked up, began to clench his fist—preparing to fend off the two men bent on arresting him. The confrontation grew tense that he could hear his heart beating louder. Then his instincts took over; his eyes narrowed, and his posture straightened. He thought of this predicament and rehearsed the same scenario in his thoughts. He was accustomed to this, he was trained to kill in hand-to-hand combat; a fluid reaction of pure instinct to counter any act of aggression. As he lifted his arms, the two men reached back to their handcuffs, ready to pin him down. The moment was tense but slow.

Just then a man yelled out, "Officers!' the old man hollered from the far side of the terminus. The two men stopped on their feet, turned, and looked. The man waived at them. "A little help here?"

Marlon, fully anticipating the takedown, turned to the man. It was the same old man he met the previous night. He squinted, slightly curious, but he was surprised to see him standing at the end of the terminal, calling the officers. The officers heeded the old man's call and approached him. They talked briefly, nodding in agreement. Marlon could not make out their conversation. He just noticed the officers nodding at the old man.

The officers tipped their caps and bid the old man farewell. Then they turned and walked off the terminal, then drove off.

Marlon was a bit surprised, quite confused of what transpired during the critical moment. For some reason, the old man was able to convince the two men to walk away, leaving him unharmed. There was no inkling or hint of any hostilities from the old man, nor a hint of any tension between them. The old man simply said a few words to the men, and they proceeded to leave without rancor. Marlon was eager to talk to him. He walked over to the old man who stood by the edge of the platform.

"What did you tell them?" he yelled.

"Would you like to know?" the old man replied, hinting no desire to indulge him with a brief dialogue. The old man began to walk away.

"Yes! As a matter of fact, I would like to know. You just used that Jedi mind trick, and those two never even said a word. They simply walked off!" He paused, smiling at the old man. "Do you know them?"

"In a sense, yes. I know them very well."

Marlon came closer. "Do they know you? Cause from the looks of it, they didn't even shake your hand or patted you. If they know you, how come they didn't even say a word in reply?"

"You are your father's son." The old man chuckled.

Marlon's curiosity peaked. "Um…I never mentioned anything about my dad.' He paused and looked at the old man in the eyes. 'Do I know you? Have we met? You're speaking to me in riddles, and I would appreciate it if you can be more direct, like…who are you?"

"Actually, you did mention your father to me last night." Marlon's face was flustered. "*This old man is crazy. If not, then he needs serious help,*' he shook his head. '*Only on public transportations.*"

"You need my help." the old man replied. 'That's why I came to you. To help you find your way."

"You're something else, old man!" Marlon backed away. "I would like to amuse you further and play along with your little charade, but I've got more important things to do. You…you do what you need to do. Just don't waste my time."

"Very well, you won't find your father here. You must find him at the terminal in Atlanta. He needs your help, and you must get there soon… before it's too late." The old man walked away.

Marlon followed him as he turned the corner of the end of the terminal. "Wait! You didn't tell me your name. Why are you helping me?" He walked briskly to catch up. As he turned the corner, he called out to the old man. "What do you mean it's too late?" Without missing a step, he glanced at his watch briefly, then looked up. But the old man disappeared. He glanced around, but no one else was present. *"What is this? This is ridiculous! That man just disappeared out of thin air. He couldn't have possibly just walked that fast. That wall is at least fifty-feet long."*

He kept looking, he checked on the cars parked nearby and peered at the trees behind the parking lot. There was no door, no window to the terminal, just a path paved in white gravel on the side of the wall. He waited for a minute, hoping for the man to appear, but the man simply vanished.

As he walked back to the rail line, his phone rang.

"This is Marlon."

"Marlon, this is Charles. Where's Pops?"

"I don't know, Charles," he replied in disdain. "He's not here. I've waited for him all night, and he ain't here."

"What do you mean he ain't there? He's supposed to be there by now! Were you late?" Charles replied bluntly.

"No...I've been here since last night around midnight. No one was waiting, and no one came. The first train arrived this morning, and he never came out. He was never on that train."

Charles was irate. "Well, did he call you?"

"No. You think that if he called me he'd be lost?" Marlon was indignant. "Call him! Then call me."

"Marlon, listen. You have to call him. I've texted you his cell phone number."

"I know, Charles. He's not answering. I've left several messages, and he's never returned my call."

"You need to find him. You need to do it soon."

"How?" Marlon raised his voice.

"I don't know. Do what you need to. Do what you have to. You're a damn ranger! You guys are trained for this!"

Marlon shook his head. "Charles, listen to me."

"No! You listen here, little brother. You are responsible for him now. You need to find him. I don't care how you do it. Frankly, I don't care where you find him. Just find him and do it soon before something bad happens."

"Well, you need to tell me his route, Charles. I can't believe that you just sent him here, telling me at the last minute, expecting me to pick him up now. And now I have to find him? This was your doing, Charles. You should have asked me!" Marlon paused briefly. "I don't know where to start, but you gotta give me somethin' so I can go where he's at."

"Do you think I wouldn't tell you if I know where he's at? Listen, Marlon, I have two kids that I got to take care of, little kids who need my attention. I have a huge—no, large congregation that I have to attend to, and I have a wife that's on my case about Pops. I'm tired of this. I don't need any more burden. It's your turn to take care of Pops. You've been away too long, and it's your turn, Marlon. You can't turn your back on this just as you did before!"

"Don't pin this on me, Charles. You have no idea what I'm going through."

"Wait! I thought you're a Green Beret? You're telling me that you can't handle more responsibility? Did you just tell me that you're not responsible? No! No! You're responsible for Pop's condition. Ever since Mom died, he's been on decline, and it's all because of you. You brought Mom to the grave," Charles yelled.

"Are you serious, Charles? You're really saying this? Listen, Mom died because Pop drove her crazy! You and Pop! He made her who she is, and you made it worse by neglecting her when she needed you. Tell me, Charles. Where you there when passed away?"

"Oh, and you were there to be her support, right? You were there when she asked to see you lying at her deathbed? Were you?" Charles shouted.

Marlon kept silent. He was stunned to hear his brother berating him. He couldn't find the words to respond to such a question that carried a heavy burden. He paused briefly, then folded the cell phone back into his jacket. He walked back inside the terminal, feeling insulted he was blatantly swearing as onlookers stare in disgust. He was livid. *After all this, after all the sacrifices I made, domestic and abroad, this is what I come home to? Ungrateful, self-righteous jerks! Why am I doing this anyway? I don't owe them. They owe me. They all do!*

He walked begrudgingly inside the terminal, hoping and wishing to find the police officers so that he could find a reason to vent his anger.

He walked right up to the ticket booth and noticed a long line of people waiting in idle to purchase their tickets. As he approached the lady at the booth, he was ready to explode in tirade. The lady, aware of the same man who came in earlier, grinned cordially. "Did you find what you're looking for?" she asked politely.

"No," he asserted.

"Well, would you like to purchase a ticket?"

Marlon paused for a moment. He couldn't decide whether to step aside and let someone else take his place or to purchase a ticket.

"Sir?" she asked softly. She was more polite than earlier.

"Um…sure, give me a ticket."

"Where would you like to go?"

Marlon shook his head. "I dunno, whichever is the quickest way to Texas."

"We don't have a train heading to Texas until tomorrow morning. Would you like to purchase a ticket heading to Birmingham, Alabama?"

He perked up, surprised to hear the lady's offer. Then his eyes furled. "Did you say Birmingham?"

"Yes, there's a train this afternoon departing for Alabama. Would you like a ticket for that?"

Marlon's anger subsided as he pondered on the old man's remark earlier. He thought about the trip for a bit, unresponsive to the lady's question. The rest of the passengers waiting behind him grumbled.

"How much?" he asked her as he pulled his wallet.

"One way? Or roundtrip?" she asked as she typed on the computer keyboard.

"Um…roundtrip."

"One or two tickets?"

Marlon was a bit concerned. He was frugal and thrifty. He didn't want to waste any money for a spare ticket if his father was never there. If he purchased two tickets and realized that his father made his way to Atlanta, then the money he saved would be wasted. He pulled out some cash and counted.

"How much for one ticket -roundtrip?" He unfolded the bills.

"It's one hundred and five dollars roundtrip."

"What? That's a lot of money for a short trip. I could drive up there for a whole lot less on gas."

"But do you get to sleep?"

"I don't care about sleep," he replied, slightly agitated.

She smiled facetiously. "You look like you could use one."

Marlon was in no mood to indulge her perkiness. He just needed the ticket. He preferred to be left alone, not to be annoyed by anyone, at least not until he reached his intended destination. He took out his credit card and paid the lady for the roundtrip ticket. His options were limited. If he drove to the station, they could possibly cross paths. He saw a better way of taking the train where he may yet find his father waiting at the terminals on the way. The train was departing that afternoon at one o'clock. He had to wait for another three hours to see if his father would arrive before he departed for Atlanta.

The small terminal had limited seating. Passengers waiting to embark stood idly by along with others who lingered on to fetch the arriving passengers. The terminal bustled steadily with people passing through. He was surprised to see that so many people chose to take the train instead of driving. Women with their children, old men who were too weak and too old to drive, young people who didn't have a license, and disabled persons unable to drive—they were all waiting for their next train. He stood out among the crowd; his height and his built garnered some unwanted stare. He knew that people constantly glanced at him, and his paranoia grew. He began to wonder. But he was unfazed. He was seething, irritated by his current circumstance. He wanted to be left alone, and he shook off the unwanted glances. He reached down to his pocket on the side of his jacket and pulled out the orange prescription bottle. As he twisted the cap, he felt something bristling beside him. He was petulant, slightly ambivalent to indulge.

"Are you here to pick someone up?" someone asked, but Marlon didn't hear the soft voice. Again, a gentle voice emerged from the noise. "Mister, are you here to pick someone up?"

He couldn't ignore the question, and he closed the white lid and snuck the small bottle to the left pocket of his trouser. Then he glanced around and then looked down and noticed a little girl sitting beside him, waiting with her mother, who was fervently digging through her purse. He was quite amused to hear a little child asking him a question.

"Are you here to pick someone up?" She smiled.

She wore an old worn-out pink shirt-a size smaller for her age. Her long blonde hair carelessly weaved in a ponytail was held together by a small pink bow that hung precariously on the side. Her pasty skin revealed a hint of malnutrition, which caused her big baby blue eyes to protrude. The mother was very young, a girl in her early twenties, a beautiful Caucasian who appeared anxious and out of place. She didn't notice her daughter striking an innocent conversation with a stranger in the terminal.

He couldn't resist her from prying. Her charming demeanor and innocent query tampered his cantankerous mood. He looked down and looked up before he offered an answer. He noticed the mother cracked a smile.

"Beg your pardon?" he whispered gently.

"You're here to pick someone up, aren't you?"

"Oh, no...I'm here for the train," he responded with a slight grin.

"Where you going?

He scoffed, "Ha! Good question. I am heading to Birmingham?" He paused. "Do you know where that is?"

"Is that somewhere close?"

He smiled. "I think so, I think it's close."

"Can you run to get there faster?"

He chuckled. "I don't think so. If you do, you will get really tired. But I'm taking the train to get there so I won't get tired."

"Oh!' She taps her mom in the arm. "Mommy, are we going to Buhmingham?"

Her mother smiled, glancing at Marlon. "No, sweetheart, we're going to Ohio."

"Why?" she asked.

"Well, your grammy lives there, and she wants to see us." She hesitated. "We're going to stay there for a while."

"Does Gammy know we're coming?"

"Yes, she does, sweetheart, and she'd be excited to see us."

Marlon, smiling, looked at the mother. "Cute kid," he said.

"Thank you," she replied politely.

"How old are you?" he asked the little girl.

"I'm four!" she blurted. Her soft, high pitched voice endeared her to him.

"Four! Wow, that's great. So, how many is four?"

She lifted up her right palm pointing all four fingers. "This many!"

"That's great. You're very smart."

"You know…I have a daughter who's a little older than you. She'll be six pretty soon."

"What's her name?" the mother politely asked.

Marlon was apprehensive. He didn't want to answer, but the little girl was looking intently, waiting for a reply. "Her name is Ensleigh."

"That's a beautiful name," the mother replied.

She gently tapped her daughter on the shoulder. "And your name, young lady?"

"Sweetheart!" she eagerly replied. Marlon and her mother laughed.

"No! What's your *real* name?" the mother insisted.

"Harpor!" She whispered and turned to Marlon. "But Mommy calls me sweetheart."

Marlon winked at her with a slight grin. "Well, I don't know. You look like a sweetheart."

She pouted. "I guess," she replied. "What about you? What's your name?" She asked. "Marlon." He smiled.

Tilting her head, "This is Mommy," she said. "Her name is Ashley. Mommy, this is Marlon." She smiled. Marlon gently shook the mother's hand, then looked down at Harpor and shook her hand.

"Where in Ohio are you headin'? If you don't mind me asking."

"Dayton," the mother replied.

"Really! I went to college in Ohio, at Cedarville. It's about twenty miles from Dayton."

The mother nodded and smiled without reciprocating.

"Are you from Ohio?" he asked.

"No, I'm from Georgia. I've actually never been to Ohio."

"Oh, well, I hate to say this, but the weather in Ohio…can be brutal. It can snow anytime during winter and rain any day during summer. The snow can be harsh, and it goes sideways."

"I love snow!' Harpor blurted. 'Mommy, can we play in the snow when we get there?"

"Sure, sweetheart. You can play in the snow as much as you want. Now, get some rest."

Harpor looked at her with a sad face. Her beautiful eyes glistened under the bright fluorescent lights. Her helpless gaze softened his heart. Sensing the mother's aloofness, Marlon felt inadequate to help them. His timid attitude brought on an awkward silence. He looked at his wristwatch and noticed that he was still a few hours away from departure. He quietly smiled at the girl and slouched on the seat to catch a brief respite. All the while Harpor grew restless and hungry.

"Sweetheart, I'm sorry, but I don't have any more to give you. My purse is empty and I...well, I'm sorry." She paused and sobbed quietly. "You'll just have to wait until we get on the train. I'm pretty sure that they have some snacks ready for us."

"But, Mommy, I'm hungry. Do you have any more gum?" she prodded her mother with her charming, droopy eyes and pouty lips.

"I'm so sorry, sweetheart. You ate the last one," she replied gently.

Marlon leaned in closer. He looked at the girl, and he couldn't resist her pouting face. He grew concerned and patted his pockets to look for anything edible. Lunch was fast approaching, and he was famished. And this brought on a perfect moment to offer his service. When nothing edible was stashed in his pockets, he looked around to find a vending machine or convenient store to purchase some food for the mother and her adorable daughter. The girl slumped over to her mother's lap, sobbing gently. Marlon felt her deep sadness from such hunger.

"Excuse me," he asked the mother. "I hate to ask you...but—"

"No, its okay," she replied, her face distinctly revealed a strong sense of apprehension.

"Well, I couldn't help but notice that your daughter is hungry. I...I was just about to grab some lunch since my train won't be leaving for a couple more hours. Is there anything I can get for you and your daughter? I mean...if it's okay with you."

"Oh, you're so kind...but I...well, I don't have any money with me, and I just spent the last dollar for our tickets. We wouldn't want to impose."

"Oh, no, not at all! I know that this is awkward, but I don't mind. In fact, I just have some extra cash and," he paused briefly. "I want to do this. So, please allow me to buy you two something to eat, and something to drink. I was planning to get something to eat since I have a long travel, but I don't want it to be awkward. And please, don't take this as a pity help. I'm not into charity giving. This is just my way of saying thank you."

"Are you sure?" she asked.

"I'm positive." He smiled. "Better yet, why don't you join me?"

Harpor sat up. "I want to go and eat, Mommy."

Marlon looked at her and smiled. "I can use some company. Lunch is better with three people sitting at a dinner table."

The small, quaint cafeteria was barely empty. Ashley and her daughter sat down as he ordered their meal. He ordered several items for the mother and the daughter to ensure that they have food to eat during their trip. He wanted to care for the mother and the little girl and his parental instincts triggered a response. As he sat down, he brought a tray full of sandwiches and desserts wrapped in clear plastic. Then one of the servers came and brought in several cans of soda pop for the mother and her daughter. The mother was surprised to see stacks of sandwiches-her eyes widened in amazement. She hasn't seen this much food stacked in a wide tray.

"Are you going to eat of this?" she politely asked.

"They look great, don't they?" He smiled. "I can eat a sandwich, but anything more than that really slows me down."

"Wow!' Harpor exclaimed. "There's so much food, Mommy. Thanks, Mister Mahhlon," Harpor said, mincing his name.

"You are most welcome, Miss. But, around this table, call me Marlon."

"Then how are you going to eat all of this? You must be really hungry."

"Oh, no! Ha! I'm not that hungry. These are for you and your daughter to take.

It's going to be a long trip."

Blushing, she replied, "Marlon, you don't have to do that."

"Oh, don't worry, I wanted to do this, as my way of saying thank you."

"Thank you...for what?" she asked with a curious look.

"Thank you for making my day. Your daughter, she made me smile again."

She responded with a cynical stare with furrowed eyes and tilted head.

As they ate, Marlon noticed several people walking by, staring in disgust. Some passed by slowly and sneered. Marlon realized that sitting with a young Caucasian woman was highly suspect for many people in the terminal. The thought never occurred to him until people began to take notice of the cultural taboo with false assumption of an interracial couple. After a while, he grew calloused to the uneasiness and shrugged it off.

He needed to help the mother and her daughter, and the gesture was more important than his own humiliation.

The woman grew anxious when she noticed some people snickering. She grew more uncomfortable sitting alongside him sharing the meal at the table. Marlon noticed her restlessness, fidgeting on her napkin and twisting on her seat. Marlon sensed that this needed to end to protect her dignity. He lifted his wrist and glanced down at his watch.

"My husband used to do that," the mother said.

"Used to do what?"

"Looks at his watch like that, flipping his wrist-as if he was hiding somethin'."

Marlon interest peaked and leaned closer across the table. "Tell me about him?"

The woman hesitated. "Well, he was a former Marine, a Recon. He would do that at every hour. It became such a habit for him to look at his wristwatch like it was his own child. He never went anywhere without it. That watch was so important to him. Its strap all worn-out like that." She pointed. "I knew that there was something about you, your strange quietness and posture. You guys are quite aloof, serious, and closed off.

Marlon recognized the common personality trait, but refused to indulge it. "Marine recon, wow! That's quite a profession." Marlon paused momentarily, wondering if he should attempt to divulge any of his own military exploits. "Is he deployed now?"

"He…um, he died three years ago. He was killed by a roadside bomb in Iraq. He was starting his third tour, and a week after he got there, he and his team were hit. All of them died when they hit a roadside bomb."

Marlon kept silent.

"Harpor never got to know her father because he was away for long duration.' She sobbed quietly. 'She was only three when he died."

"What's his name?" he asked softly, his voiced cracked.

"Charlie. Charlie Robinson," she replied with sadness. Her face revealed utter disdain.

Marlon remained still, unsure of his reply. She was a stranger, and she needed to be consoled. But he felt awkward and strained. He felt the pain of loss, and refused to pry into her personal life. There was no consolation with the tough, hurt-filled past. He felt a tremendous sense of sympathy for a young mother to have endured the loss of a husband who suffered unjustly under such cowardly act of an invisible enemy, an enemy with wanton thirst to maim and kill those who stood and fought for a noble cause. He knew the sacrifices made. He understood the laws of war. The unintended casualties on both sides. But the heinous acts and shallow disregard for the sanctity of life that thrives without boundaries were beyond comprehension. The thought of unimaginable acts inflicted to the innocent continues to elude his reasoning.

Again, he felt awkward in response, feeling that there was no sense in justifying such loss. There were no quaint answers to be offered to a grieving widow living the sudden loss of a husband and a noble soldier, no simple gestures to lift the hopes of a young mother struggling to provide. But Marlon felt the sense of loss, the shame of justifying a political cause. And he knew that nothing thrives beyond a man's quest to conquer his fear and satisfy his thirst for violent means. He pitied her, but he knew that his consolation is insufficient and benign.

He looked at Harpor, her dulcified face beaming as she devoured large pieces of bread, stuffing every corner of her mouth without restraint, oblivious to her surroundings. But she felt her mother's sadness despite her mother's futile attempts to hide her prolonged grief.

"Attention all passengers! Train departing for Cincinnati will depart in ten minutes!" The crackled voice came off the loud speakers hanging from the ceiling. After the second announcement was repeated, Ashley hastily packed up the food as she was getting ready to leave.

"Thank you so much! You've been so kind. We appreciate the food." She paused and took her daughter's hand sitting in front of Marlon, hoping to stay linger to see them through. "Harpor! We have to leave, sweetheart. Our train is about to leave."

Marlon nodded in reply.

"The food was great, and it looks like we'll have more than enough to get through the day…God bless."

Marlon stood up, slightly ambivalent. "I'm truly sorry for your loss…for your husband's death. He's a good man. I've met and came across Recon Marines while I was deployed in Afghanistan. They're tough, fearless, and crazy, but Marines through the core. They were the consummate professionals. He died for a good cause…doing something he loved alongside his brothers." He paused for a few seconds as she stood motionless. "I lost several men under my command and its tough…losing those you loved and cared for! Not a day goes by that I think about them. Their faces are etched inside here." He pointed at his temple. "I still blame myself for their death, wondering if I made the right call. Sometimes I'm not sure…if I was supposed to die and they were supposed to live, but you do what you do, given the choices you have, and you…well, you move on."

"My husband died for his country…and his brothers, but he left me and his daughter behind. Now I don't know what to tell her…'cept that her father died fightin' for this confused country. You can call it noble or just, but it doesn't soften the pain. This country robbed me of my husband and her of her father." Her voice crackled.

Marlon felt such a strong pull of bitterness, an inconsolable grief reserved only to a young widow. But he couldn't blame her for the anguish, the sense of hopelessness and uncertainty. She was entitled to her bereavement no matter how long or how deep it consumed her.

"I am truly sorry for your loss. I want you to know…that your husband's passing was not in vain. He's a hero, and you and your daughter, especially your daughter, must know the sacrifices you've made and the life he offered for his buddies. She must know that her father was nothing short of a hero. He fought and died. And not many could have done what he did, and you should be proud of that. I hope that you will find comfort wherever you go, that you will find peace-that God will comfort you as you grieve and find solace after this tragedy."

Then she quickly got up, clearly distraught and annoyed. "A hero? A hero is served for the worms!" she said. Then she took her daughter's hand, nodded at him, then walked straight to the terminal.

He stood by the table, and smiled gently waving his right hand as he bid farewell. They rushed outside and boarded the train. Harpor glanced back and waved. "Bye, mister!" She smiled as her mother pulled her away. The mother turned to him and waived with a straight face.

"Bye! It was nice meeting you," he hollered. He kept smiling until the girl was out of sight. Then he slowly walked back to his seat as the train began to leave.

He looked at his watch and noticed that he still had an hour to wait for his scheduled departure. As he waited, he thought about the girl. Then he pulled up his wallet from his coat pocket. He flipped it open and noticed the photo behind his driver's license. It was a picture of his young daughter, its glossy clear finish was faded, its' creases worn, but her innocent smile remained vivid. Her effervescent face still refreshing despite the faded glossy finish. After a brief moment he began to sob. *It's been a while*, he thought. *"Here I am wondering about the father and his daughter. She will never have that chance to see him, no chance of touching him, kissing him, hugging him. She will never see him again. He will fade from her memories as time passes. She will never get that chance to bid him good-bye. And he will never see her and walk her through the aisle. He will never be that father she needed."*

He wiped the small tears from the side of his face, sniffing, as he slipped the photo over his driver's license. Her effervescent face was refreshing despite the faded glossy finish. He waited and sat back down, then slowly closed his eyes as he slipped into a slumber.

Chapter Nine

Dawn descended swiftly as the warm sun rays pierced through the cracked windows straight into his eyes. Unfazed, he kept staring at the faded rusty-stained, popcorn ceiling. He had hoped for a prolonged respite, wishing to gain a brief shut-eye before the alarm blared off after the light. His eyes shifted from one side of the bed to the other, searching for a way to a steal some semblance of sleep.

The past that raced through his thoughts throughout the night kept him awake and despondent. His eyelids were heavy, and his face flustered. He closed his eyes for the third time only to be awakened by the clanging noise of a rusted clock sitting next to a black rotary phone over the old wooden night stand. Then the phone rang. He looked at it but ignored it until it stopped ringing.

After several minutes had past, the phone rang again. This time, he turned and picked it up. "This is your six o'clock- wake up call. Please press zero if you have received this call." The automated voice repeated until he pressed zero. He slowly placed the phone back and sat up on the edge of the bed. He wiped his face, scratched his scruffy chin, and breathed a long sigh. "*No sleep! Maybe I'll catch some sleep on the train,*" he thought. He walked over to the adjacent bathroom next to the entrance. After half an hour, he walked out of the hotel room, dressed in the same attire from the previous day, carrying his suitcase. He walked over to the concierge and requested for a taxi to shuttle him off to the station.

"How was the stay, Sir?" the attendant smiled.

"The clock, it was broken," he mumbled, still groggy from the restless night.

"Oh, my apologies. We didn't know. But thank you for telling me. I'll get someone to fix it right away."

"No trouble. It was actually…comforting." He cracked a smile.

The attendant was a bit bewildered at his reaction. "Well, I'm glad you enjoyed your stay," he said as he hands him a piece of paper. "Come back and see us again. I'm sure the clock will be good as new…if not new."

"Thank you."

The phone rang, and the attended went on to answer. Just then, the police officer entered the lobby.

"Good morning, Eli!" the officer blurted.

He was surprised to see the officer from the previous encounter steadily approaching him. He didn't expect that he would follow through his promise.

He replied with a curious look. "Good morning!" he said "You look confused," the officer smiled as he shook his hand. "I…I wasn't expecting to see you again."

"Well, I promised you that I would pick you up in the morning, didn't I?"

"I don't recall, but this is quite a surprise."

"Are you ready?"

"Yes! I was just about to call a taxi, but it appears I won't be needing it."

The two exited the hotel and drove off on the patrol car heading to the terminal. The day was fast approaching; the sun beamed much brighter than usual on a fall season. As they drove off, Eli was mesmerized by the breathtaking colors etched in the sky; the magnificent splendor strewn across the vast expanse cast over the vermillion horizon that receded under the auburn clouds. The clouds faded to fuchsia all randomly patched under the blue plane.

"Such splendor," he muttered.

"Beautiful…simply beautiful," the officer whispered.

"I have never seen such amazing display…like a wide canvass filled with nameless colors indescribable by any earthly definition," he muttered softly.

"Only an imagination can achieve such artistry,' the officer replied. 'It's a sign Eli. It's a good sign."

"It's just the sky!"

"It's a sign, just like any other signs you see drawn up. It's as simple as a street sign. You know you've made it to your destination when you see the street sign. It tells you where to turn, and it tells you when you've arrived."

Eli remained quiet, reflecting on the man's simple analogy. "I guess. It can be a sign, but a sign for what?"

"Have you ever seen beautiful things on your journey in life?" He paused and turned to Eli. "You know, the good things you see in life. The beauty of your child's birth? The beauty in your bride's eyes. That beauty in your salvation? You know when you have a good thing coming."

Eli nodded.

"It's not hard to spot a good thing when you find the beauty in it."

"You're getting too deep for me."

"Wait! Don't tell me that you're just brushing this off! C'mon, Eli, you can't deny it. There is beauty in the things that you've experience in life all those years."

"I can see it, but I'm not following."

"You're wife, wasn't she one of the most beautiful people you've met? The good things that followed the day she said 'yes' when you were still trembling after you asked her to marry you?"

"It was a good thing," he whispered.

"And you're children. You're two boys. It was a beautiful thing, that day you held them in your arms for the very first time. Good things came of that."

"I agree."

"Well, this is the same thing…there! In the skies, you haven't seen such beauty, such splendor scattered right above you. I bet you've never seen a picture as beautifully orchestrated in such a random moment, have you?"

Eli shook his head. "No."

"Well, guess what, good things are about to come,' The officer smiled. 'I know good things will come your way."

"I hope you're right. I hope that there is some good news that will come about."

"If you are hoping for a silver lining, I don't want to bear the bad news, but they do not exist."

"I'm not looking for silver lining. I'm just looking to find my way back and see my son."

"Yes, I know. But you're also, no…you've always looked and hoped for that silver lining. Something that has eluded you all your life. What was it?"

"You know, you may be the most philosophical man that I've ever met."

"Don't change the subject now. You and I both know what I'm talking about."

"I know, I know." He paused and slouched. "It's been a good life. God's been good to me." Eli said. The officer replied with an amiable smile.

They arrived at the terminal a bit later than anticipated. The conversation took longer as the officer drove slowly. Both men paused and reflected. Eli appeared seemingly eager to part ways. The officer grinned as Eli shook his hand and exited the car. Eli stood up, turned, and smiled. "Thank you for the ride, Officer. It was nice of you to drive me around. I must admit, I have never met a police officer who is as kind and caring as you. I really appreciate the help…and the talk."

The officer tipped his cap. "You're welcome, Eli. I'm glad that we have spent some time getting to know each other. Who knows, maybe we'll bump into each other again. I have a strong feeling that we'll meet again."

"That would be nice," Eli replied and waved good-bye and entered the terminal.

"Eli, I'll see you soon!" the officer yelled out as Eli kept walking. Eli, hearing the officer's call, glanced back and smiled.

As he entered the building, he immediately walked over to the billboard. A terminal employee was standing nearby. "Where you headed?"

"Atlanta!" He replied confidently as he looked up the black billboard.

"Looks like your train is 'bout to leave.' the man pointed to the train. "Got your ticket?"

"Of course I do,' he snidely replied. "I got it last night." He patted his back pockets. Then he tapped his jacket. He appeared confused. *"Now where could that ticket be?"* He began to panic, frantically digging through each pocket.

"Eli!' someone blurted. 'You forgot something!" Eli turned and noticed the officer walking briskly approaching him. "Here! You forgot your ticket." The officer smiled as he handed him two passes.

"Thank you,' he replied. 'But I only need one."

"Well, you'll need the extra one…I'm sure."

"Thank you again, listen, I would like to stay talk, but my train…it's leaving," he replied timidly "Be safe, Eli." The officer waved good-bye as Eli walked off and boarded the train.

"Wait!" Eli turned. "I didn't get your last name…to thank you," he said.

"Miller, my name is Sam Miller," he said as he waved good-bye.

The train was packed. Each car was full of passengers heading to Atlanta- passengers from a wide gamut of social strata. But the majority of them were poor, people who couldn't afford a plane ticket for their trip or drive a vehicle. Some were simply not capable of driving. Each section had four seats facing each other on each side of the aisle. People were chatting obnoxiously, babies were crying, and some were fighting through a seasonal cold; coughing and sniffling. There were many single mothers with young children and infants ambulating between the seats, and children running rambunctiously up and down the aisle.

Eli searched for his seat, dodging children along the aisle. When he found his seat, he noticed that no one else was sitting, a vacant section on the front of the car. When the train began rolling, no one else came by and sat down with him, only a small black boy sitting behind him who stood up in front of him, then turned and smiled.

"Hi!" the boy blurted.

"Good morning!" he replied softly.

"Hi!" The boy smiled.

"Hello!" he replied with a smile.

"Knock, knock!"

Slightly mused, Eli asked, "Um…who's there?"

"Knock, knock!"

"Okay…who's there?"

"Knock, knock!" he asked the third time.

Eli, sensing that the boy was asking without any inkling how the joke was to play out, smiled at the little boy. "Hello, what's your name?"

The boy smiled blissfully, oblivious to his query, repeatedly asking the old man with his knock, knock jokes.

"Quincy! Please, sit down, child!" his grandmother who was sitting next to him, prodded. The boy smiled again and sat down.

The woman stood up, turned and looked at Eli. "Pardon me, Sir. He just foolin' around. Boy doesn't really know how to finish these jokes," she chuckled. The elderly woman appeared optimistic. Her eyes were tiresome, but gentle-her face exuded a strong sense of resolute, and her smile revealed some semblance of peace and wisdom. Her thick black and silver hair settled on the sides of her head that parted under her white cap, an ostentatious hair piece that hung loosely on the top of her head which she held on with one hand as she held on to the boy with the other.

"Oh, no! It's no trouble at all. Funny kid, he reminds me of my son, full of energy and personality. I find it quite amusing. So please, don't apologize." He paused and smiled at the boy peering in between the seats. He winked at the boy. "Quincy, huh?"

"Yes, his father named him after Quincy Jones," the woman replied. "He got plenty of energy. Yes, sir. So, you'll have to excuse us if we get fussy. We gonna to keep it down. Right, Quincy?"

The boy nodded quietly.

"Are you heading to Atlanta?" he asked.

"Yes, we are. We're headin' out to see his father."

"Are you his grandmother?" he asked, implying that she was a bit advanced in years to have a little child.

"I'm his father's mother, so, yes, that would make me his grandmother," she chuckled.

"I'm on my way to Atlanta, to meet my son as well. He's a bit older."

"I see. Does he live in Atlanta?"

"No, he's in the military. He's just pickin' me down there. I actually do not know where he lives. I've never seen his place. Haven't seen him or his family for quite some time. He's been deployed several times, and I'd like to go and visit, if my health permits,

but I have a feeling that I won't be seeing him for quite some time after this. What about you? Are you just visiting your son or…"

"Yes, Quincy and I visit him once a year." She paused and leaned closer. "He's been in for quite some time," she boasted.

"Oh! I'm sorry, I didn't mean to," he conceded.

"Oh, no, it's okay! I'm used to it. He's made his choice, and bad choices come with severe penalties. But I'm glad that he's doing all right. At least he won't be able to hurt no one." She turned then sat down.

Eli, slightly curious, prodded her. "I'm curious. Why would you say that?"

She slowly stood up and turned to him. "Well, I'm not too proud to say this, but the boy, well, he had a lot of rage, yessa!" She wagged her finger.

"Uh-huh. Lots of rage inside that boy's heart. I ain't proud it. I tried to raise him the best way I know I could. You see, his father walked away from his family when the boy could barely walk. He's grown up without a father his whole life, and as his mother I was working at least twelve hours each day to put food on the table. No one's around to watch him. He got into joining gangs and all sort of nasty stuff. I prayed hard for that boy. I never stopped loving him." She paused, her eyes glossed in sadness. "Sometimes...all there's left is prayer. All you can do...is pray. When they grow you'd hope that they grow up to be successful, to be a man of integrity and a godly man. You're hoping, no, you pray that they'll turn out good! But most times, you can't make them choices, they grow up to make their own. And without proper guidance, their compass can point at the wrong direction, taking the path of least resistance. It keeps piling up. And the stuff that they don't understand can lead to unimaginable rage. Children can be molded into what you would like them to be, to be a good man o' woman, but in the end, they have to choose. You guide them however, and where ever you like them to be, but in the end, they has to walk through them doors, yessa! The path they take can lead to incarceration...if they lucky...or a wooden casket, if they so foolish."

Eli nodded in agreement.

"How long's he been in there?"

"Just when the boy turned one, he'll be there for quite some time. Lord knows if he'll change. He says he is a changed man, but a desperate man will say anything to sweeten them ears. I just don't want the boy to miss out and not know his father. Good or bad, he needs to know. Hopefully, he'll learn from his father's mistakes and choose the right path, just like your boy."

"Well, my boy was a hard shell to crack, but he turned out okay...I guess."

"Mister, if your boy's not inside an eight-by-ten, he good," she whispered. "He's served his country, he's not being served. Its' betta' to give than to receive! But you know what? We can't choose our children. They come with all sorts of blessings and imperfections—just a smidge on the paint or a crack in the porcelain. For a good God to give us a great gift he gives us the ones to give us joy; ones that make us cringe, and ones that makes us glow in amazement. Our children can bring us down to our knees so we inch closer to heaven. Just the way he sees fit for our sake. An' all we can only pray, an' hope that the ones we raise turn out good."

Eli nodded. "I appreciate your honestly."

"Oh, it was nothin'," she replied with a smile. "The train's about to move, I betta' sit down. Okay, good talkin' to you."

"Likewise," he replied with a slight grin.

He slouched back against the sturdy chair. Its cushion, worn out from repeated abuse, and its cracked leather surface, subjected to prolonged neglect, creaked with the slightest movement. As the train moved faster, the buzzing sound of the rail tracks beneath his feet and the repetitious movement of the insipid flatlands lulled him to sleep despite the ruckus around him. His destination was five hours away, and he could not resist the urge to make up for the previous night. The prolonged travel has taken its toll on his body and his mind couldn't piece everything succinctly. But the sleep ignited blissful memories of youth as he sank deeper into his dream.

Chapter Ten

A distinct, midnight-blue ford sedan zoomed in haste and passed him on the packed road, almost clipping him on the side. If it weren't for his quick reaction to avoid contact, he would have been badly hurt. But that did not faze him as he kept a keen eye at the lady across the street. Several minutes earlier, he noticed a young woman passing by, inches from him. And from that moment on all his thoughts were jumbled, his stomach churned, and his feet felt light, and his movement felt smooth. He was ambivalent at first, but grew desperately eager to meet the beautiful girl across the street. *"I just have to see that girl,* he thought. *I need to get her name."*

He hesitated at a moment; he knew that he was not in the right position to approach her; the timing wasn't right-it wasn't the right occasion. No woman should accommodate any man still dressed in drab, dirty working clothes. He was still on the clock and he could not afford to waste his boss' time. His attire was inappropriate for the moment. His approach would be deemed insulting to a formal lady. His scruffy jaw and his frizzy hair were unflattering to a prissy young woman dressed for a Sunday service. It was Sunday afternoon, and he was working tirelessly under a strict foreman. This was an untimely moment to offer anyone for a trifling preposition. Nevertheless, he boldly approached her.

"If I don't say something, I may never see her again. I've been in this place many times, and I have never seen her before. I just have to say hello. If I greet her, she may tell me her name. If not, heck at least I got to look her in the eyes."

He hesitated for a brief moment. "Excuse me. Ma'am?" he blurted as she walked past him.

She ignored him as she crossed the dirt road heading to another store across the street.

"Miss?" he called out to her once again. This time he was beginning to sound more assertive and intrusive. She glanced back, then walked briskly toward the closest door, but she missed reading the sign hanging over the lintel. She peaked through the door to see the man following her before she proceeded to close it. She saw him approaching the steps, walking with a swagger. Then she quickly closed the door and flipped the locks to prevent anyone from entering.

He saw the door swing shut. Then he looked up at the sign hanging on the lintel and smiled. He noticed that it was quite unusual for her to enter a bar. He was surprised to see the sign. His eyes grew wide and his cheeks blushed, he was completely embarrassed. He found it quite amusing for a young black woman unwittingly entering a watering hole exclusively frequented by white middle-aged men.

He came closer by the crack of the door and poked his head by the window. He looked inside and hesitated for a moment, then walked past the door and waited for her. Since he was crunched for time, he returned to the feed store across the street to finish his errand.

After skirting away from his purview, she took a second glance over the window and noticed that he was backing away and looking indecisive. Everything behind her was quiet, only the dimmed fluorescent lights seemed lively that hovered over the dark place revealing the shadow faces of its patrons; most of whom are white, middle-aged men. Soon after she took a deep sigh, someone behind her cleared his throat, and she was immediately startled. Much to her surprise, she gingerly walked backward and turned slowly. She saw a man standing right behind her holding a beer mug, his right hand snuggly resting inside his front pocket. He was embarrassed and perturbed to see a young black woman entering an exclusive establishment reserved only for his kind. She noticed bar patrons sitting by the counter drinking with their eyes fixed on her. The bartender, an old white man, stood behind the counter with a demeaning stare with his arms tucked in, and his face turned pink. He took a deep breath and proceeded to ask, "Young lady, why did you enter my establishment?" he asked.

She noticed every patron sitting nearby were dumbfounded, staring intently with disdain and amazement. She cleared her throat and raised her chin. "Umm…my apologies, I wasn't…I didn't know that this was not meant for a young lady like me. Beg your pardon, Sir. I'll be on my way now." She pointed to the door. "Thank you for your hospitality." She paused and stood quietly for a response, hoping to redeem herself from further humiliation. She was afraid of what may transpire and smiled politely at every person whose eyes remained fixed at her.

"Well?" the man spoke. "Wanna have a drink?" One of the old man sitting at the bar asked.

She shook her head without uttering a word.

"Shut up, Carl! You don't make any decisions around here. You've had too much!" The bartender replied with a chastising tone.

"Young lady, did you see the sign outside?" the bartender asked.

"No, sir," she replied softly.

He shook his head in disbelief, quite perturbed of the awkward moment. "Well, you don't belong here. This ain't a place for young girls as your kind to enter. Colored folks ain't welcome here."

"I'm so sorry, I best be on my way." She frantically unlocked the door, unable to unlatch the bolt.

"Geez!" the bartender yelled as he walked out of the counter toward her.

Her embarrassment slowly turned to fear-to be caught inside a louche establishment, especially on a Sunday afternoon, was frowned upon. Someone as formal, young, and naïve should not be caught in a precarious place. This was not the place nor the time or day to be inside a bar—a place reserved for white men. So she hastily exited and turned right, looking straight ahead.

Eli immediately noticed her exiting the bar after he heard the door bang shut. He turned and resumed his approach and walked briskly to catch up. "Miss. Please, wait!" he called out.

Sensing that he was following her, she immediately walked in straight into an old grocery store.

The store clerk greeted her by the door. "Good afternoon!"

She glanced to her left and noticed the clerk standing behind the counter, stocking the shelves behind him.

"Oh, hello. Good afternoon, sir!"

"Can I help you?" he asked as she walked up to the counter pretending to shop. She had no intention to purchase any merchandise. She hesitated for a moment as her eyes restlessly shifted from one end to the other.

She remained quiet, waiting for Eli to walk past the store. She saw him through the large glass window walk by. But then, just as he was to disappear from her sight, Eli stopped and peered through the glass.

"Miss? Is there anything that I can…get for you?" the clerk.

She appeared fidgety. Then he noticed Eli looking outside in-his hands cupped over his cheeks as he leaned against the window and the store sign.

She was embarrassed, hesitant to indulge the man. After a brief silence, she could not allow any lingering silence and arouse the man's curiosity. "Sir, I may sound out of place, but that man outside.' She paused. 'Well, that man…he's been following me for quite some time from the feed store. Scary lookin'."

He leaned closer. "Who? That boy, Eli?" the clerk whispered.

She nodded.

"Oh, don't mind him. He's a good boy! Probably came here to run some errands from the lumber yard. Ol' Man Boley sends him over once a while to fetch some goods for him and his crew. He's harmless. He may appear uncouth, but believe you me, miss, he's no threat to you or me."

"He looks…undone," she replied.

"Uh-huh! Oh, I get it. He fancies you!" the man replied, grinning as he waved at Eli and invited him in.

"Believe you me, that boy is quiet, shy, and timid. You'd barely hear a word from him. He's polite. But sometimes, I wonder about him. 'Tis hard to get a word out from him, Ol' man Boley tells me that he's got a motor-mouth when no one is around. Quite strange for a young fella."

Eli noticed the clerk inside talking to the girl. The clerk gestured for him to enter. Eli was acquainted with the store clerk since he was a young boy. He ran errands for his father before he worked at the chicken coop. As he entered, he greeted him with a casual nod. He was polite and shy. He did not utter any word to the man standing behind the counter, oblivious to his greeting. He zeroed in on her, determined to meet her, and nothing else seemed to matter. Everyone seemed invisible. He was completely enamored by her beauty, and he couldn't resist the urge to ogle at her. She was frightened, and her ambivalent mood grew apparent each passing moment.

"Eli, come here, son! I want you to meet this nice young lady." The man paused as he leaned closer to her. "Your name, miss, if I may?"

"Caroline," she replied softly.

"Caroline, I want you to meet my friend, Eli."

"It's…it's good to meet you, miss. I…I just wanted to tell you that.' He froze with a dumb look.

"Well, son, spit it out!" the clerk blurted out.

"You're beautiful!" he blurted.

She was shocked. No one has boldly complimented her in the open. The young man's brevity and pointed statement thawed her icy disposition. He was persistent, and no one seemed to have taken the liberty to teach him proper mannerisms. This was unusual for him, and she was surprised to see his audacity. Eli didn't stop there. He followed her to the store. He simply refused to let her slip past him. This was an opportune moment that never occurred, and he wasted no time. His intentions were clear, and she was caught unguarded where she was obliged as it was customary to act formally when greeted, especially for one prissy damsel.

"I…I need to leave. Time is short," she replied, pulling her hand away. "It was nice to meet you, mister," she said timidly.

"His name's Eli," the clerk interrupted.

"Nice you meet you, Eli. I best be headin'!" She walked briskly toward the exit.

Eli stood quietly, slightly amused. He was grinning from ear to ear; his eyes drooped above his hanging jaw.

"Eli! She's leaving, son!" The clerk poked him on the shoulder. "Don't let her go, son. She may never comeback."

Eli was still in daze. "Um…what do you think I should do?" he asked.

"What's your gut say?"

Eli was dumbfounded. He was desperate, eager to pursue, but fearful of the outcome. He paused for a bit, then walked towards the exit.

"Son, whatever you do…from this point on, the choice you make can and will change your life." The man added as he leaned closer with both hands on the counter. Eli nodded in reply, then quickly exited the store.

As he exited, he noticed her walking briskly toward the street corner where an old woman was waiting by the car. She was quite young, barely in her forties. And he paid no attention to her concerned look. He walked faster, chasing after the young lady who was briskly walking towards her car.

"I don't know what else I should say," he thought. He finally caught up to her at the street corner as she greeted her mother. He halted, hoping to avoid the awkward approach and remained cordial. Then he sheepishly approached them in a casual manner, hoping to deflect any hint of desperation. But her mother knew his intentions, and she was predisposed to abstain from this growing nuisance. As he came within reach, he felt a sudden, soft twist inside his chest-something he's never felt until such an indelible moment.

"Hi, my name is Eli," he said confidently, extending his hand to offer a handshake.

She looked at him and looked down on his right hand. She remained quiet and annoyed. "Yes, I know your name," she replied tersely.

Her mother looked on, straight at him, sizing him from the top of his head to the tip of his worn-out boots. Her eyebrows were furrowed. "Boy! What you doin' here?" she asked him with a chastising look.

"Good morning, Ma'am. My name is Eli, Elijah Coe." He gently nodded.

"Good morning?' she answered. 'It's afternoon. You come here to chase my daughter? Well, you can forget about it."

"No...no, Ma'am. I just wanted to introduce myself, in...in case I see her again."

"You betta' run, boy! We ain't interested...whatever you sellin'. Y'er wastin' your time here, and from the look of it, you ain't got nothin' good to offer."

"I'm not selling you a thing. I just wanted to meet your daughter," he replied, pulling his hand back to his side.

"I know your name, Eli. I'm Caroline. I'm sorry, but Momma and I have to leave," she kindly replied.

"Well, I hope we meet again." He smiled.

They proceeded and returned to the parking lot Eli looked at her and waved his hand. "I'll be here next Sunday...same time." He smiled.

Caroline shook her head and grinned slightly, amused by his persistence.

Right before they entered the car, her mother looked at her and gave her a wry stare, shaking her head in disbelief. "You stay away from that boy! He looks like he's up to no good. You best listen, or I will lay on you!" she said as she nodded in fear.

As they drove off on a rusty brown Buick sedan, Elijah looked intently at the speeding vehicle, walking after their wake with his hands tucked inside his pockets. He kept staring at the car as he stood in the middle of the narrow road. He was surprised to see her slowly turning her head, gazing at him from the rear window until she disappeared from sight. He waved his hand and smiled as he stood erect at the middle of the road until they were gone. Then it began to rain. Small droplets that suddenly poured heavily on the small town, but he stood there unabashed, and completely soaked from head to toe. One of the cars passing by nearly grazed him. The driver did not notice him until he came within reach; he swerved to the side, honking his horn. He was perturbed at the young man standing unwittingly at the intersection, undeterred by the rain and the passing cars.

Eli walked back to his truck, confident and excited, prancing and dancing in the middle of the street as onlookers gawked in amusement. He was in high spirits and completely excited of what transpired that day—when time seemingly froze when she walked through that door. He's never felt such deep desire for a woman, and he was smitten by her charming, graceful demeanor. As he drove off, he has completely forgotten his initial errand. His mind wandered off—daydreaming of his fortune that slowly unfolded. As he sped off, he kept looking for the brown sedan, hoping to see it and dream of her. But Caroline and her mother were nowhere to be seen. When he finally came to his senses, he immediately turned and rushed back to the feed store, loaded his truck then sped off.

As he looked around, he noticed the transport truck barreling through the middle of the road. He pumped his brakes and honked his horn to warn the other driver, but the truck didn't move. Just then, he swerved to the shoulder before he came to the bridge, the truck's side rail hung precariously on its side that slung over the median. Its driver slumped over the wheel completely asleep, but his foot remained on the gas. He was hauling logs of freshly cut pine trees hanging precariously on the side of the truck bed. Eli kept honking his horn, but the other driver did not budge. As the truck came in fast, Eli swerved off to the shoulder to avoid a deadly collision.

As he crossed the bridge, he noticed that parts of the wooden rail to the left of the bridge were missing. He slowed down, slightly curious, to see what caused a rail to dislodge. He checked to see if there was anything parked on the side of the bridge or over the side of the bridge, but no one was present. All he saw was the strong muddy water crashing underneath. He felt something amiss and the missing railings appeared unusual. Nevertheless, he kept on driving.

As he blared the radio louder, he realized that he had completely forgotten his errand for old-man Boley. He unwittingly left town and missed his supply run from the feed store. He jerked the wheel violently to his left, and hastened back to town. As he passed by the bridge, he noticed that the water rose dramatically from the heavy rain. He was running late and he couldn't spare any time to waste to head back and run over. He slowly drove over the bridge. When he opened the window to wipe off the rain, he heard a loud, strange noise—sounds of rushing water splashing against metal. The noise came from under the bridge, so he decided to stop and check. He parked on the shoulder and walked over the bridge. He glanced over to his right at the foot of the bridge, but nothing seemed out of the ordinary. He trotted at the other end, but everything seemed normal. Then he heard the creaking sound as it grew louder. He heard pieces of metal bending and glass breaking. The heavy sound of rushing water sifting through a metallic object was distinct; its high-pitched clanking noise could only mean that something or someone fell off the side of the bridge. Out of concern, he jogged toward the side of the missing rails. When he made it to the edge, he noticed the murky water and the rushing river current crashing violently into the rusted silver rear bumper of the Buick sedan with its license plate protruding above water—almost all of the car was swallowed as it sank beneath the murky current. He couldn't believe what he was seeing. His heart sank as he watched the car sinking under water beneath the bridge.

Chapter Eleven

"Pardon me, sir," the man stood by his side and tapped his shoulder. Eli slowly came to his senses, his eyes were heavy and his vision was foggy. The dream had ended abruptly. He looked up and noticed a man standing to his left, looking straight at him. His piercing crystalline-emerald eyes appeared gentle, his unblemished face glowed, and his smile was serene and inviting. His commanding presence emanated with radiance in an ominous space. Eli looked at him and cracked a subtle smile. The man nodded, and Eli completely understood what he was implying. So he sat up and tucked his left elbow to accommodate him.

"Thank you kindly," the man added as he sat down. Eli, slightly annoyed by this interruption, looked at him briefly.

"Much obliged," he replied. Then he looked out the window.

"These aisle seats, they're tricky aren't they?" he said.

Eli nodded and smiled.

"Just can't tell when someone runs you over so you have to watch your elbow."

"True, I know what you mean," he replied. "Tell you what, why don't you switch seats with me. I've sat by the window for quite too long. Frankly, it gets old."

"Do you mean the view? Or are you talking about sitting?" the man asked.

"The scenery gets old…not much to see."

"Well, I appreciate that," the man gently replied.

Eli slowly got up and squeezed his way toward the aisle. The man got up and sat down by the window.

"Thank you for your kindness," he said, looking at Eli. 'The view looks great!' He smiled. 'First, I woke you up, and then I took your seat. Thank you for your kindness. My apologies for the trouble I've cost you."

"Oh, no, no, it's no trouble at all. I needed to get these legs moving. Stretch out and get the blood flowing."

Eli sat down, breathed a sigh a relief and sunk his shoulders to resume his sleep.

"Where are you headed?" the man asked. Eli opened his eyes and looked at him.

"Atlanta," he muttered softly.

"A relative," the man said.

"I'm moving in with my son. He'll be waiting for me there when I arrive.' He paused. 'And you?"

"Same place.' the man replied. 'Except that I'll be meeting him there."

"Loved one?" Eli asked poignantly.

"You could say that.' The man paused. 'I don't think he knows that I'll be there, waiting for him to take him home."

Eli was curious. He looked at the man and tilted his head. "Don't mean to pry. You're heading there and the man whom you're supposed to meet doesn't know your coming?"

The man nodded subtly. "Exactly!" he uttered. Eli leaned back and refused to indulge the man any further. He reclined on his seat and closed his eyes, but after several minutes, he opened his eyes, sat up, and looked at the man who was looking out the window. "I'm curious," he said. "Does he know you're coming?"

"No," the man replied subtly.

"He doesn't know you're coming, but you're supposedly going to meet him there?"

"That's correct."

"Then, how does he know you're coming? Does he know who you are?"

The man grinned. "Yes, he knows who I am, but he has not seen me in person. And he's not expecting me to meet him there," he replied.

"So…he doesn't know you're coming, and he doesn't know who you are. And if he's not there to pick you up, and you're there to fetch for him, then why the terminal?"

"It's where he needs me."

"He needs you?' he asked with a high-pitched voice, shaking his head. 'I'm sorry, but you're confusing me."

The man eyes twinkled. "There's a point and time where the journey will end. That time is near."

"I'm not following."

"It's simple. He longs to see me, and I'm coming to take him home.' He kindly smiled. 'It's time for him to go home."

"Where's home?"

"It's not the time for me to reveal that?" The man chuckled.

Eli nodded. "Fair enough."

"Tell you what, when I get there, I'll introduce you."

"Have me met?' Eli asked abruptly. The man remained silent. 'I guess not," he added.

"My name's Eli.'He candidly offered his handshake. 'What's yours?"

Just before the man was about to reply, a train conductor came and stood by next to him.

"Tickets please," the train conductor asserted.

Eli dug through his chest pocket and took out the ticket, and handed it to the conductor. The man sitting next to him took his ticket out and gave it to the conductor.

"Looks like you folks are headin' the same place," the man added, clipping the ticket stubs.

Eli glanced over the aisle and noticed that all the passengers were fast asleep. No one seemed to care or pay any attention. The car was engulfed in silence, not even one person could be heard talking or snoring. Then glancing back, he noticed that the man sitting next to him was staring back at him.

The man smiled and asked, "How's your dreams, Eli?"

"How did you know I was dreaming?"

"You were talking in your sleep while I stood next to you."

"That bad, huh?"

The man nodded his head, smiling.

"Well, I was actually dreaming about the past," Eli replied.

"Please, kindly tell."

"Well, I dreamed about the day when I met my wife for the first time. I could barely remember it now that I'm old, but my dreams…they were clear as though they happened just yesterday. My wife and I met when I was in my late teens. She was younger than I was, but quite mature for a young woman, funny how we met. I came across her at the middle of the street and chased her around until she stopped. An old store clerk introduced us, and that was when he told me that my life would change forever. I didn't know what he meant by that. I guess I was too caught up in a moment when I stood right there, as close as I could get in front of her. I wasn't thinking then. Everything around me faded away, and I was mesmerized." He paused and slouched back on his seat. "She actually ran off. She told me that I frightened her." Eli laughed.

"That's quite a beautiful moment," the man replied.

"Oh, it was quite a day. As I drove off to return to work, I realized that I had completely forgotten my errand. So I decided to return to the feed store and fetch supplies, and when I came back, I almost got hit with by a truck. I swerved to the side before I came to the bridge. When I came across a broken railing at the bridge, something inside me was telling me to stop and look, and I did! That was when I found her and her mother sinking at the bottom of the river, trapped inside the car. I didn't think. I just had to jump." Eli paused and shook his head.

"Well, did you jump?"

"I wanted to, but I got scared, and just before I jumped, I squatted down and saw several large boulders all over the river, just under the water. I didn't know how, but I just noticed them. So, I rushed down to the end of the bridge at the shallow end and swam to the car. By the time I got there, the water level had risen up to her neck. I tried opening her side of the door while under-water, but the door won't budge."

The man's eyes narrowed. "So, how did you get it to open?"

"She was frantic, woke up from the rising water inside the car. She pushed the door out, but the door wouldn't open. Then I pointed to her, when she saw me outside her window, and I told her to roll down the windows. She didn't listen because she was panicking. But after a short moment, after trying so hard to open the door, she decided to roll her window down, and by that time the water was over the vehicle. When she rolled the window, I immediately pulled her out and took to the riverbank. We barely made it, and we were almost out of breath. After a brief moment, I went back in and dove down to the car. By this time, the car was completely submerged, and I was losing time. When I got down to the car window, I saw her mother lying inside, lifeless."

"Her mother did not make it," the man implied.

"No, she didn't make it. By the time I got there, she'd already drowned, and maybe if I got there sooner, I could have saved her."

"How come?" the man asked.

"I…" He looked down. "I got scared. I wanted to save her. That was the right thing to do."

"But you didn't, did you?"

Eli shook his head. "No! I…I wasn't…" He replied with a pensive look.

"You did what you could with the time you were given."

Eli's face turned doleful. "I still wonder through this day. Caroline… well, she was hysterical. She had a difficult time recovering from this sudden loss. She had bad dreams for many years. The traumatic experience left her scarred. Her immense grief was only surpassed after the birth of our first child."

"Losing a loved one after a tragic accident is difficult. Moving past the loss when you felt responsible for the death carries guilt and heavy burden. No person should carry that burden alone."

Eli breathed a long sigh. "I'm sure that she's with her mother now. She's in a better place."

"I agree.' The man paused and leaned closer. 'Do you miss her?"

Eli looked at him with yearning eyes; his eyes exuded a sense of deep longing to be reunited. "Every day," he replied softly.

"I'm sure that she's waiting for you. But you'll have to wait. Patience can take a lifetime."

"In my case, it won't be that long. I'm aged and advanced in seasons, and I look forward to the day."

"Which day is that?"

Eli looked at him with a sense of hope. His eyes glistening with joy. "The day when I see her again."

"You seem to be more excited to see her than to see your son."

"My son doesn't even want anything to do with me."

"How can you be so sure? Isn't he waiting for you at the terminal?"

"He's supposed to meet me there. But I won't be surprised if he ain't there."

"I'm certain that he's there."

"You believe that?" his voice cracked.

The man gently closed his eyes and grinned. "Yes, I'm certain that he'll be there." He paused then looked out the window. "Question is, are you ready to meet him? To hold him once again?"

Eli was apprehensive, confused of the man's blunt question. His eyes narrowed. "Honestly, I don't know. My son is not too fond of me, and he's made that known."

"When was the last time you saw him? Or hugged him?"

"I don't recall. Could have been during his college graduation."

"That must have been quite some time. How can you be sure that he doesn't want to see you?"

Eli shrugged his shoulders. "Parents' know these things. But I think he still blames me for his mother's passing."

"Your son, Eli, may not come across as the best kid in the world, and I can see that you love him, but he wants your love more than ever, since you took that mantle from your wife. Every child desires that from their parent. No matter how old they become. He wants to forgive you, but you have to forgive yourself and reconcile. He may be lost, but so where you, and he needs you."

"I know my son. He's a good kid…a great kid!"

"I'm certain that he needs you…more than you know."

"You seem know him more than I so," he replied, slightly suspicious.

"I would like to get to know him, and for him to know me," the man asserted.

"He's a hard-headed kid. I still can't figure him out to this day. I doubt I'll ever get to."

"No parent, no matter how wise they are, will ever know their children, no matter how old they become. And that's one of the greatest irony of parenting."

"How so?"

"Well, every child is different. They are unique in each and every way. When you place two fallible people together, you'll bear fallible children. Each one has a part of you, but each one must choose their own path. That is the way of life in this fallen world."

"Just have to ask. Do you have any children?" he asked.

"I do!"

"So, you know…the pain, the heartaches, the disappointments, all the joy crushed when they leave you, when they lose their own way."

119

"But I also know the insurmountable joy that comes with it…when they smile, when they laugh, when they hug you, when they say they love you. They are unique in their own way. There is heartache in this life. That's the beauty of humanity and children. They're the purest symbol of a father's love. No man, unless he brings a child into this world, will every come close to feel the way God feels about his children. Being a parent is a great blessing given to humanity. Bearing your own children is a perfect illustration of pureness and innocence rolled into one. The love it bears is a taste, a glimpse of God's grace."

"I've never thought of it that way before."

"You recall the days when you raised your two boys?"

"Yes, I do. I still remember, not many good memories, but I remember the best ones."

"And the bad?"

He hung his head. "It's harder to forget those."

"You chose to remember those…the bad things. And it bothers you."

"No, I doubt it."

"The bad things will happen and they happen, but it is does not define who you are because they were meant to pass. But the past sins passed down corrupts the soul and perverts the heart. People, especially children, will make mistakes. It's up to us fathers to guide them through the right path. Eventually, they will have to decide for themselves which path to take. But it is our task to impart wisdom so that when they come across that difficult decision, they will know which path to take. The source of all wisdom will grant us the right discernment that we impart to our children, when we fall short.

"Hmm, that is very interesting."

"You tell me that you have grown old and long in years, and you chose this path, but I want to tell you that loving someone, forgiving them, choosing to embrace them is not old-fashioned, and it's never late, and natural. It is sublime. It is the piece that molds us stronger. It never gets dull. You carry a heavy burden, a sense of guilt from your wife's passing and the apathy bore by your children. Why?"

"My boys loved their mother more than they loved me. I can see that now, but I had no choice. I worked long hours-six, sometimes seven, days a week. Sometimes I worked on Sundays, just to keep up with the rent and the bills. I wanted to spend more time with my family, especially with my Caroline, but I had to pay the bills, and they never understood that. You're a man, a father. You know this."

"Do you love them?"

Eli bristled at the man's intrusive question, "What kind of question is that?"

"It's a simple question," the man replied softly.

"Of course I do! They may think otherwise, but I know in my heart that I loved them with all I had. Heck, I worked long hours just to put food on the table."

"Then why does it bother you?"

Eli was annoyed. "I'm not bothered at all. The boys just never understood."

"Children will never understand the way you display love. It's the most important affirmation they need. You love your children, but money does not make up for lost time, and time was not intended for that. And you will never get that back."

"Easier said," Eli replied.

"If you chose to hold on to those, you will lose your way."

"It's too late for that." He asserted.

"You made up your mind, and you chose not to let it go. You conditioned your heart to be calloused. You bear a weight that was more than paid for, but you continue to harbor the ills and regrets long past. The chasm has grown deeper and wider between you and your boys."

Eli remained silent, unable to reply to the man's statement. As they kept silent, the boy in front of them started to cry. Her grandmother calmly eased his fussiness, whispering gently.

Looking at the child, the man asked. "You know what I like about children?"

Eli shook his head.

"Children want to forget easily.' He paused briefly. 'They love with such abandonment. They desire honesty, believe innocently, and forgive blissfully."

"I hope you're right." He smiled.

"You doubt me.'"

"It's pretty obvious, isn't it?" he whispered.

"You're holding on to something you would hope would soothe your heartache, and you're resentful that it remains elusive."

"There's nothing wrong with that."

"No, it will elude you when your hope is misplaced."

Eli leaned back. The train whistle blew, and the next terminal was nearing.

"Tuscaloosa, Alabama. Well, here's my stop!" the man said.

"Wait! I thought you're headin' to the same place as I am?"

"Yes, I was. Right now, I'm needed here, and I have to go.' The man got up and skirted his way to the aisle. 'I'm sure sure I'll bump into you again," he added.

"Well, it was good to meet you. I hope we meet again."

"Cheer up! Soon, you'll be seeing your son. It will be a joyous occasion."

"I...I hope so. Good day to you, sir."

"Thank you. And you as well." The man walked over to the exit in front of him, and as the train came to a full stop, he stepped outside, turned as he waved farewell.

Eli smiled politely and waved quickly as he sat by the window, staring intently at the man standing at the terminal. As the train began to move, Eli gazed at the man until the man was out of his line of sight. "*I hope he's right.*' He slouched back. "*I hope that my son still needs me. What an odd man.*"

He went back to sleep, hoping to rendezvous with past dreams disrupted by a serendipitous occasion.

Chapter Twelve

"This is going to be a long, painful trip." he thought as he sat down on the first row. He had one more stop before reaching his intended destination. He glanced at his watch and rolled down his sleeve. "Three hours up, three hours down, then it's off to another six-hour drive," he muttered. No one else heard or noticed him as he slouched back on the worn-out seat.

"Business or pleasure?"

Marlon looked up and noticed a man sitting across from him leaning by the large window. He remained quiet for a brief moment, slightly perturbed and hesitant to respond. The man appeared out of nowhere, and he was fairly certain that no one was sitting at his row when he sat down, nor did he notice anyone skirting his way to the window seat.

Marlon cleared his throat. "Umm…neither," he snidely replied.

He laughed. "It must be personal then."

"I guess. I'm sorry, and you are?" he asserted.

"Oh, I'm just here for a visit."

Realizing that he was unable to avoid the conversation, he relinquished his indifference toward him. "Good to meet you then." He timidly waved his hand. "I'm Marlon."

The man replied with a gentle nod. Marlon took out his orange prescription bottle and opened it, tapping a couple of capsules to his right palm. The man looked at him intently. Marlon looked away and swallowed the pills without any water.

"Does it help?" The man interrupted.

"A bit." Marlon smiled.

"That's not my question."

"It helps me. That's all you need to know," he blurted with an annoyed stare.

"How many of those do you need?"

Marlon's eyes narrowed. "Listen, I don't know you, and you, asking me very intrusive question, it's quite insulting."

The man chuckled and sat up. "Fair enough," he replied as he rested his palms on his knees.

Marlon stared at the man intently, quite curious at the man's pointed question. As he gazed on his hands, he reminisced of a past encounter he once had during his last mission. *'Déjà vu. Those hands…they look the same.'* Then he looked up and noticed the man's eyes. *'Strange,"* he thought.

"Have we met?" He blurted.

"When would that be?" the man replied calmly.

"Your eyes, I'm sorry, but you remind me of someone I…I…once bumped into. This sounds creepy, but there is something about those eyes, looking at them made me feel whole. I've never felt such powerful presence of love until the moment I've looked into those eyes. Just like the ones I saw from that man in the desert."

The man smiled. "Oh, where was that? Please, tell me."

"It was…in Afghanistan."

"That would be a different place, rather far, don't you think?"

"Yes." He smirked. "I don't forget faces and I don't forget a man's eyes."

"If I was in, as you said, Afghanistan, then why would I be here?"

He chuckled. "I dunno. You tell me."

"How did this man appear to you?"

Marlon hesitated momentarily. He knew what happened, but couldn't piece it all together. So he divulged pertinent information in order to glean from the man's insight on the tragic incident that occurred that fateful day in Wanat. "Well, he was fairly tall, white guy, white beard, not typical for any Afghani. And his face…they were unblemished, smooth and fair. And his eyes, well…they were green…like a dazzling jewel. I've never seen those colors, easy to remember, but hard to describe. I've looked for those colors, and nothing came close…until now. I never forget those eyes."

"How did you meet him?" the man whispered. His eyes was piercing but engaging.

"Oh, I've never met the man.' He paused. 'My team was sent to recon the nearby village to find and kill someone. But before we got to the village, we came across a narrow pass and noticed a man. That man stood at the middle of the road. He was holding the leash of his burro. He stood there, unmoved, like it was his territory, and no one, not even the dog, dared to challenge him. It was as if he came from another place and commanded such a presence. It was strange, peaceful, but strange."

"Then something happened."

"Yes, something happened. When we came around and passed him, after a good distance, he disappeared, not even his donkey was there. He was gone that fast. But he stood there, and we couldn't understand why. No man in my unit dared to aim their weapons at him. It was as if he was in control, and no one dared to challenge him. It was quite powerful, and I've never seen anything like it, nor have I encountered someone as commanding." He leaned closer. "Later that day, we found out that the engineers found an IED buried exactly where the man stood. It was buried so deep that the explosive ordinance disposal teams blew it up with a pound of C-4's. It blasted a huge crater that could have decimated the two Humvees, including mine."

"Who do you think that man was?"

"I can't tell you if I knew. Maybe…" He shook his head in disbelief. "Maybe he was an angel, or God in the flesh."

"Would you have believed him if he had told you?"

Marlon shook his head. "You know what, I would have."

"It is easier to believe."

Marlon shrugged his shoulders. "I doubt it!"

The man leaned closer. "Is it difficult to have faith?"

"It's not for the lack of it. I've seen the worse. And faith? It goes out the window when bullets zing past you. Belief, that's what we had for each other. And hopelessness made us invincible. Over there, we were gods, but here…we're alone fighting an unseen, unending battle. Believe me, I've seen the worst of people. And I can tell you, a man will pray to anyone, Buddha, Krishna, Mohammad, Christ. You name it, he'll pray to any god he could just to wiggle his way out beneath death's grip."

"Well, someone prayed for you. That's why you are here."

125

Marlon tilted his head. "I guess someone prayed. I don't know who called out to God, a man whom I barely knew. I don't think he feels me. I don't understand the meaning of faith."

"Don't you need faith in your friends, your family? As a matter of fact, it was there, in your time of need where your faith was and is being tested. But your doubts had clouded your judgment and brought you to ruin. That's why you have questions that need to be answered."

"So, you're telling me that you can answer my questions, right?"

"Why are you here, Marlon?"

"Wait…I've heard that question before, at the station. The old man, he…"

"So, answer me."

"My pops…he needs me."

"It's more than that."

"I don't know how to answer that. I know that my father needs me."

"You said that, but why are you here?" The man pointed his finger at him.

Marlon's face grew flustered. "I just answered your question. You didn't catch that, did you?"

"My question is simple. Why are you here? I'm not asking you for a reason. I'm asking you for an answer."

"I'm not following you."

"You're here because you want something. The past continues to haunt you, and you can't find a way to escape. You're bitter, and you blame yourself and those around you. You're lost, and your distance had brought a wide chasm between you and everyone else, including your father."

Marlon was stunned to hear the man's candidness and his face turned pale.

"So, let me ask you again, why are you here?"

"Honestly, I don't know," he whispered.

"You have lived long enough under the cloud of darkness. Your reclusiveness has hardened your heart. You turned into a hollowed instrument—a grieving soul. You must go and find those that are close to you. Forgive yourself. Forgive your dad. Forgive those offenses. Leave the past.

Step outside of the dark. And stop looking back. Forgiveness is not for them. It's for you, so that your heart will heal, and your soul awakened.

When you live your purpose and gain peace, you will know that God has never abandoned you."

"Seems very important. Quite a message you got," he bristled.

The man nodded, sensing his sarcastic tone. "I'm not here to keep records of the past. I'm here to offer hope. To give you life, a hope and a future."

Marlon sat there quietly as he deeply pondered the man's pointed revelation. He hesitated to engage the man further, and he was not fully convinced. "Let's play this along,' he replied. 'Suppose you have a message for me. What is the message?"

The man looked him in the eyes. "Your father is waiting for you at the next terminal. You must meet him there. He's frail, he needs you badly. His time is coming."

"Wait, I've never told you about Pops."

"Why do you dwell in the past?"

"I did not tell you about Pops."

"No, and you don't have to. I know you, and you are stubborn. I know about Cheryl, about your daughter, Ensleigh, and the men you've lost under your watch. I've named you before you were born, and I have walked beside you through your darkest days."

Marlon was taken aback, unsure how to respond to the man's remark. "I didn't have much in me left. I have nothing to offer. My daughter doesn't know me because my wife doesn't want anything to do with me. My marriage failed because she couldn't understand and chose not to understand. And my dad…I just wanted to earn his respect."

"Don't try to find what is no longer there. You can't expect people to understand, or give you what you need. You pushed your wife and daughter away. You couldn't fathom the guilt that you carried, for your men and you felt bitter. You wanted to place the burden on her for your marriage. And it was easier," he added. "You daughter needs you just as you need my help. You are the one who must learn to cope and understand. That forces that are out of your control must be offered on the altar of grace."

Marlon was adamant. "I don't even know where to start."

"The beauty of grace is that it cannot be measured within time. Choosing the right path does not hinge upon the right timing. It does not depend on time, and it has no boundaries. You must choose grace. Your wife will forgive you, your daughter will forgive you, your father will forgive you, but it begins with you. It is a gift that is given without expectations."

Marlon began to sob quietly. "Why did I fail?"

"That is not up to you to decide your fate. You're here, and you kept on. You are not a failure, only searching."

"I'm responsible for those men. I am responsible for those innocent lives. The children. Those innocent victims and their families. I know I was part of something evil, for what Framm did to those people."

"There is no depth for any evil. Framm made his choices, and he chose to repay evil with evil. But in the beauty of the ashes, hope prevails. "

"Why did it happen?"

The man didn't answer. He smiled and gave a deep sigh. "I'm here for you because your mother asked me, and I know that you want, you want... you want answers."

Marlon leaned closer. "Why?' he asked. 'Why would you allow innocence to be trampled?"

"You must choose righteousness, and do not repay evil with evil. Man is born with evil intent. That's why I came and died for it. I am not of this world, but the world will live under the rule of evil until its rebirth. I will judge. My word is truth. It is eternal. And my promises will prevail. The cries of the innocent will be avenged, and that time will come."

"But...why? Why am I here? How did I get here? I did what I could with what I was given. I...I made the right choices to serve and to lead. I gave up my life for my men. You have to tell me. How did I get here?"

"Your life begins each day. Stop searching for answers. You've followed orders for so long. It's time to follow me and turn this world. Your life in the past does not define what's to come. You made wise choices for your men. You've relied on your training all this time. Now, you must rely on me. Have faith in me. Stop blaming yourself for their loss. This is the time for every man to repent, and their time will come when they draw their last breath. Your path has been paved. Your destiny is awakened. Don't look back, or you will find yourself standing—a pillar of salt. You are blessed, and you will bear a testimony for me to those who grieve. I know the plans that I have for you. Plans to prosper you and not to harm you, plans to give you hope and a future."

"My mother recited that verse to me when I was a child. I never forget that verse. Let me ask you something, and excuse for prying, but what's going to happen to me? Please, tell me."

"The time will come when you will have your answers. But you must choose. Believe and have faith."

"You're not telling something that you already told me."

"You will find yourself when you come home. Lay your anger to rest, bury your resentment, and you will find the reason and the purpose when you arrive at the garden of peace. Marlon, is God's love not enough for you? Is it too hard for you to believe in me?"

Marlon leaned in. The smiled subtly. 'I know what you are looking for. Just like that moment when I stood there on that ground when you and your men drove around me. I protected you at the time you were vulnerable because your mother prayed for you, asking for your safety. I heard her prayers. She has asked me to come to you to comfort you. You can choose this path and look back, or you can choose the path I paved for you."

The train arrived earlier than anticipated. As it came to the terminal, the intercom pinged twice to warn the passengers that the train was approaching the next stop.

"Ladies and gentlemen, we have arrived at Atlanta terminal. Please be advised that this is the last stop. Any passengers must disembark at this station. Any connecting departures will be posted on the terminal schedule. Thank you for riding Amtrak. Good night."

"This is my stop,' Marlon said. 'Will I ever see you again?"

"This may be your last stop, but it is only a chapter. A new chapter will begin. You will find a new purpose, peace that has eluded you, and you are favored. When you lose your life for my sake, then you will find it, a life so richly blessed."

"Please, don't leave now!" Marlon pleaded as he reached for the man's hand. When he touched his hand, he suddenly awoke to the sound of the screeching tracts.

The train conductor touched him on the shoulder as he ambulated from one passenger to the other. "Last stop," he blurted.

Marlon appeared disenchanted as he awoke from a deep sleep. He squinted and rubbed his eyes. "Sir!' he called out. The conductor turned.

'Did…did you see a man here? He was sitting right in front of me. Did you see him walk past you?"

"I haven't seen any man walked past me. No, I'm sorry."

"Are you sure? He was just here talking to me. You did not see anyone at all? He had green eyes, dark hair," he raised his hand to describe the man's height. "And he was about this tall."

"Well, unless you're speaking of an old woman and her children, I can't say I have. I guess I would have to say no, I'm afraid not."

Marlon was confused, but he refused to press the conductor any further. He looked behind him and asked the passenger sitting close by.

"Excuse me. Did you see a man here? He was sitting by me just a minute ago."

The lady looked at him with bewilderment. "Nope, sorry."

"You sure?"

"I haven't left my seat for the past hour, and you were the only person I noticed sitting there. You were talking. But I thought you were just… talking in your sleep."

"Why would I do that?"

The woman shook her head. "I have no idea. You got issues."

As the train reached the terminal, Marlon sat back and looked at the window. He noticed a cloudy imprint on the window-a smudge of the man's fingerprints. *I don't believe in coincidence. It can't be.* He looked around to see if anything gave him further proof that the man once sat there. He felt the seat, in front of him-it was warm. *I don't believe this to be coincidental.* He bit his lips in amazement.

As he stepped off the train, he turned and looked at the window and paused briefly, then his eyes widened. He remembered the man's hand. There was a distinct injury on his wrist, a sharp object that pierced through it was barely concealed under his sleeve. He smiled and walked briskly to the terminal. He noticed that it was dark outside; only a few lamp-posts with faint fluorescent lights flickering offered slight comfort. Only a few glaring lights from the vehicles waiting idly at the far end of the terminal stood still. It was difficult to see outside; people's faces were masked by the shadows of the dark that penetrated as deep as the cold air breezing through his numbing lips. He shook off the cold, breathed deeply, then he entered the station.

Chapter Thirteen

Eli arrived at the terminal earlier that next day, rested and invigorated. His face beamed with effervescence. He was eager to see his son. The anticipation has turned joyful and the angst had melted away. Sensing that his time is short, he had come to a complete understanding that this serendipitous intersection will foment a closure that has long eluded him. As he disembarked, he immediately headed inside the terminal, hoping to see his long lost son.

He browsed through the aisles, hoping to catch a sight of him; he glanced around the booth to find him. Then he worked his way outside by the parking lot, ambulating from one lot to the next. Marlon was nowhere to be found. Disappointed, he returned inside and sat down to await his son's arrival. As time lapsed, he grew worried and pensive, hoping to see him each time the doors swung open. His restless anticipation dissipated each passing moment. No one in the terminal seemed to mind him. And after three hours, he slouched on the wooden pew and slept. When he closed his eyes, he was immediately transported back into the rare blissful past.

The autumn sun remained unusually high over a receding afternoon. He was sitting by the steps of the old wooden porch he recently painted white, but the color had faded after the merciless heat and wet summer's gale peeled off small paint chips He had hoped for a peaceful afternoon after a long day's toil tending his garden under the open sun, but the random peel on the wooden floor annoyed him.

It's been six months since he savored the taste of burning whiskey. And he craved every sip, reminiscing of its strong odor. He was resolute, intent of keeping his promise to his wife, and the six-month sobriety is difficult to corral. Beneath the serenity lay a turbulent journey to find the will to battle his addiction. The fight to control and repress his self-destructive proclivity stemming from the bottom of the whiskey bottle continued to swirl, but the struggle has churned slower each day he took to stay dry and fight his demons. Deep down, he resented it, and the cravings remained reticent-despite all his gains. Yet being sober felt invigorating and peaceful-a total contradiction to the solution he once embraced from inebriation. Despite the pull of alcohol, he remained resolute, constantly occupying his mind with work and spending his spare time with the boys.

He sat at the highest step, sipping a glass of lemonade while resting his elbow over his knee. He was savoring his fresh lemonades with ice on a hot autumn afternoon. *"The boys are still gone. They should be home by now. Where are those boys,"* he asked himself.

Once the school year ends, the two boys often ventured out into the woods playing, exploring, and jostling with other kids. Their father resented this, but their mother encouraged it. He was a stern disciplinarian, and the boys never dared to arouse their father's ire in fear of swift punishment. During the summer days, when schools were closed, Eli would force his sons up earlier than the regular school days. He'd nudge the boys from their deep slumber at five o'clock. He would take them and walked with them to the church to plant and till their small garden which the church has allotted for them and other families in need of assistance. He would prod them, teach them, and continuously push them to work tirelessly throughout the day before breakfast. On their way back, he would stop by an elderly neighbor's house and ask them for any errands for his boys. The two were instructed to clean the porch, take out the trash, or fetch a bag of groceries for them. Eli continued to do this, and the boys resented him deeply. This continued on through their teenage years.

Caroline arrived at the usual time, carrying a bag full of vegetables and a worn-out black purse that hung loosely on her shoulder. She came home late in the afternoon from working as a housekeeper and a cook to a wealthy family in town. She inherited this job after her mother's passing. She toiled from dawn till dusk for six days straight. Although she was tired, she never ceased to care for her boys. She also washed their laundry. Sometimes she'll tend the children to bed. Since Eli worked during most nights, the boys were often left on their own volition to fend for their meals during the day as their father slept from a graveyard shift. The two were inseparable, and Charles, being intellectually gifted, often came to his younger brother's behest to explain and aid him with homework. Marlon, despite of his instinctive nature, struggled academically, but Charles never gave up and continued to teach his younger brother despite his brother's vehemence stemming from his learning disabilities.

That afternoon, Caroline's face emanated radiantly despite her exhaustion and lethargic feeling from a long days work. Eli noticed it as she approached the steps.

"Baby, are you okay?"

She breathed a deep, long sigh then smiled. "Oh, I'm gonna be okay," she replied as she sat down next to him.

"You sure?" His voiced cracked, as he offered her his lemonade.

"I'll be okay. Just winded, is all," she replied and shrugged her shoulders lightly as she took a sip. "Where's the boys?"

"I dunno. They supposed to be here an hour ago."

She leaned close and rested her head on his shoulder as he wrapped his arm around her. Then she spotted the boys out of the woods.

Noticing their parents sitting on the front porch looking straight at them, they looked at each other and walked briskly toward them, anxious and afraid. As they drew closer, they quickly hung their heads down, they eyes wandering about. Charles, fearing his father's ire, hunched his shoulder, but Marlon appeared calm and cocky.

"There's my two beautiful boys!" Caroline called out.

"Hi, Momma," Marlon said as Charles remained silent. Marlon embraced her and sat on her lap.

"Boy! You betta' greet yer motha," Eli blurted, staring firmly at Charles, whose head remained bowed.

"Good evening, Sir. Hi, Momma." Charles replied sheepishly.

"Come here, son. Let me see your face." Elijah grabbed his right hand and examine his son's chin. He smirked and remained silent. "Go in and wash your face. You and I will talk when I'm ready to whoop you."

Charles remained silent and entered the house.

"Hold on!" she yelled out and stood up. "What happened to your face?"

Charles was petrified; he took a step back and turned to his mother.

"Oh my! Lord Jesus! Who did this to you?" Caroline gently lifted his chin.

"Sorry, Momma," Charles replied.

"Boy, you betta answer my question. Who did this?" She looked over to her husband.

Marlon approached her. "It's okay, Momma. I took care of it," he proudly said.

"Excuse me? Took care of what?" she scolded Marlon.

"The boy who hit Charles. He was bigger, but I hit him and knocked him down."

"You've been fightin'?" she asked sternly.

"Yeah!" he asserted.

"Why?"

"I'm a man. That's what a man does," Marlon perked up.

"You a man now, huh?"

Marlon nodded in reply, his chin up high, his jaw shut and tight. "You don't go about fightin. A man does not go about fightin' for petty stuff."

"Caroline,' Eli interrupted. 'Let the boy explain. Thinks he's man enough!"

She firmly tapped Charles on the shoulder. "What you got to say for yourself, Charles?"

"He wanted my toy, and I refused to give it to him. So, he dared me to climb the highest tree, and I said no. So, he hit me."

"Why would he ask you to climb the tree?"

"To fetch his ball."

"Did you try and help him?"

"No."

"Well then, why not? You're supposed to help others when they ask you for help."

"Momma, he used that ball to throw at me and Marlon, and it was a big basketball. And when it got stuck on the tree, he got scared, and he wanted me to fetch the ball, and I didn't want to 'cause I didn't want him to hurt me or Marlon no more. It ain't right, Momma."

Caroline kept silent, worried of the boy's reply. Then she took his hand and looked straight into his eyes. "When someone's in trouble, you help him," she replied gently.

"But, Momma!" Marlon interceded, "He gonna hurt Charles."

"Balls don't hurt nobody. And if you fetched it for him, he'd probably stop throwing it at you, and he'd be your friend by now."

"But, Momma!" Marlon pleaded, his voice cracked.

"Enough. I don't want to hear it anymore. What you did was wrong, Marlon. Fightin' won't solve anythin'. You only fight when you see the helpless being bullied. Fighting is a sign of weakness."

"Well, Charles was being bullied."

"Charles needs to learn to help others."

Eli looked intently at the boys, "Okay! We're done for now. Charles, go inside and wash your face. Marlon, you and I will talk later after you wash your face. Get inside, clean up your face, wash your hands and get ready for supper. Go!" he yelled.

After the boys had eaten their supper, they proceeded to retire in the bedroom to avoid their father. As they were about to enter, their father's booming voice came through the living room. "Boys!"

They paused, glanced at each other, and rushed to their beds. They were petrified of their father. They could hear his slow rhythmic footsteps creaking louder on the wooden staircase. They hid beneath the thin blanket. As the door opened slowly, they began to cry. Eli approached them and stood on the middle of the room, between the two beds.

"Boys!" he uttered, his voice was deep but calm. "You know why I'm here, right? I told you that I will talk to you. I know you're awake. Sit up!"

The two sat up, whimpering.

"Why are you two looking like you're scared?"

"You gonna whoop us!" Marlon cried.

"And why would you say that?"

"'Cause...we done something wrong, Pops," Charles replied.

"What'd you do wrong?"

"We got into a fight," Charles replied.

Eli looked at Marlon with disdain. "Marlon?"

Marlon nodded. "I guess so."

"Boy, you better think before you speak."

"Yessa," he replied with a sheepish look.

"You did something wrong. You got into a fight. But you had every right to defend your brother. You stood up for each other, and you stood up against a bully. But fighting should only be your last resort. You don't go 'bout fightin' out of anger, pickin' fights just because you want to.

135

You fight 'cause you have to. You stand up to bullies, and you don't back down if they push you." He sat down next to Charles. "Boys, fightin' don't make you a man. Just makes you a badass. You want to be a man? You start helping out your mother around the house and listen to your father. Now, since you two boys came home late, you two deserve some punishment. So, tomorrow mornin', you two will get up at five o'clock and paint the porch."

"But, Dad, we just painted it," Charles pleaded.

He looked at Charles firmly. "Yeah! So?' Either that or you spend the morning gardening at the church."

"We'll paint the porch," Marlon replied raptly.

"Good!" He looks at Charles then whispers, "Son, you're the older brother. You're older for a reason. You gotta set a good example for your baby brother.

"I'm no baby," Marlon bravely replied.

"You are one if you act like it." Eli looks at him. "You want some spanking?"

"No, sir," Marlon muttered.

Eli walks toward the door. "All right, you two get to sleep, and don't let me hear you goin' fightin', coming home with a swollen jaw or a black eye. You hear?"

The boys nodded.

"And if you have to, don't show your mother. You'd give her a heart attack!" He shuts the door. "Good night!"

"Night, Pops," Charles replied.

Eli retired to his bedroom. There, he noticed his wife lying down, fast asleep. This was unusual for him since she typically was up longer before he fell asleep. As he sat down and reclined, she touched him by his arm. "I needed to start before you came. I'm sorry, but I'm so tired I don't think I'd have any much left in me to stay awake," she said. Eli held her hand and turned.

"You're not mad at me?"

"Fo' what?" she gently replied.

"The boys...for what they did," he replied.

"You're the father. Why didn't you lay them straight. Those two shouldn't be fightin' like they should. No good thing can come of it."

"No, those two deserve to be punished, but they did something good."

"And what's that?"

"They stood up for each other."

"But hitting don't make it better."

"It does, when you have to defend yourself."

"And where did it land on Charles? See that boy's face?"

"Bruises heal, scrapes will fade, but respect. That's hard to find." His lips curling slightly. 'Besides, the boys will learn from this, and it's a step for manhood."

"Fighin' doesn't make you a man, Eli. Just gets you in trouble. Accountability, that's what makes you a man."

"You're right, Linny, but, them boys will stick for each other now, and that's something I never had."

"You know what? Those two will have to learn to use their heads rather than their fists, and I don't want to see no bruises anywhere on them scrawny bodies."

"You gotta let them be boys, Linny. They just boys wantin' to prove somethin'. Fightin' may be no good thing, but them fists is all you got when you got nothin' else. A man's gotta stand up for somethin'."

"Get those boys doing somethin', they got to fightin' for idle hands." She bristled then breathed a long sigh. "Long day." She rested on her side then fell asleep.

"I got them workin' hard tomorrow." He kissed her on the cheek. "Get some sleep, and we'll talk more in the mornin'. Them boys will have to keep fighting for somethin', and it ain't a bad start."

She closed her eyes, unable to resist the urge to stay awake. She sighs. "So long as they fight for each other, that's all right with me. Make sure you talk to the boy's father and straighten this out," she whispered.

He closed his eyes. "Nothin' to fret. It's just part of life. Guess we'll just have to wait."

Chapter Fourteen

It came in fast and loud. He was caught in a deep slumber when he was rattled by the blaring sound of the arriving train. He was still leery and slightly delirious. He was awaken by the screeching sound of the last train. Glancing, he noticed a man approaching from the right side. He tilted his head up, placing his hand over his brow and squinted to see if he could recognize him as he gracefully glided through the aisle. The man stopped and stood under the piercing fluorescent light, his unrecognizable face beneath its glare. As he came close, Eli called out to him, "Marlon? Is that you?"

"No, Eli. It's me, Sam."

"Sam!" His shoulders perked up. "Officer Sam?" He grinned with a surprised look in his eyes. "What are you doing here?"

"I've come to take you home."

"Home? Did Marlon get a hold of you? Did he ask you to come for me?' He paused. "Wait. I just saw you five hours ago. How did you get here so fast? And why aren't you in uniform?"

Sam smiled. "You have a lot of questions."

"Why did you come? I'm confused. I'm not lost, am I?"

The man chuckled. "No, Elijah, you're not lost. Confused? Yes, definitely!"

"So, why are you here?"

"I'm here to take you home. Caroline is waiting for you. He...is waiting for you." Sam replied softly.

Eli remained silent. His eyes narrowed under a furrowed brow. "But...I, I just got here." His voice cracked. "I'm supposed to see my son."

"It's time, and your time has come. God is calling you home," Sam replied with a sobering tone.

He looked down, shaking his head. "But this doesn't make sense," he mumbled.

"Nothing in this world makes a lot of sense, but that's the beauty of heaven. Everything comes into full circle.' Sam sat down next to him without touching him. 'You have questions, and you seem worried. You're life has passed, and eternity is at your doorstep. Embrace it." He smiled. "You're worried. Why?"

"I just don't get it."

The angel remained silent. He sat back, waiting for his reply.

Elijah's eyes wandered to and fro as he fervently searched for answers. Then he smiled and slowly breathed a sigh of relief. "Give me a chance to see my boy once more. My eyes are tired, and my body is old, but what I have I want to leave it all. I just want to embrace him, to comfort him, and to tell him that I loved him."

"It's time." Sam gently waived.

Eli gathered himself, sat straight, and prepared to leave. His limbs were calm, his body was at peace, the tremors had finally ceased. He was finally free. "I've never felt the love that I've felt until now. It feels as though that time is standing still. Such overwhelming peace." His smile curled and his eyes twinkled.

"You want to say something?" Sam whispered softly.

Eli looked at him and a tear rolled down the side of his face. "You can always take me anytime. I am ready. But..." He paused then wiped his tear and dried his eyes. When he opened his eyes again, Sam was gone. He looked around to see where he went, but he was nowhere to be found. He leaned back and glanced at the large clock above the ticket counter behind him. *Nine o'clock.* Then he looked at the door and noticed another man approaching.

Marlon entered the second wooden double doors at the far side of the terminal. He was excited to see his father as he ambulated from the one end to the other. He restlessly searched for him among the crowd. When he came to the last pew, he noticed his father sitting at the far end. He appeared lethargic.

Eli looked up and noticed the man calmly approaching. He smiled, then looked away. The man came closer and stood in front of him. He wondered why he was smiling at him, staring intently. Then he turned ambivalent, he barely recognized him. The two traded glances, then Marlon blurted, "Hey, Pops!" He smiled.

Eli's eyes widened, then reciprocated with a smile. After several years, he has forgotten his son's face. Eli leaned closer, and after a brief silence, his face brimmed with excitement; he was in tears. Then he stood up, and gave him a firm embrace. "My boy!" he cried. He gently closed his eyes. "My boy," he whispered.

"Pops." Marlon whispered. "You made it."

The old man could no longer restrain himself and tears flowed from his face as he embraced him tightly. "You've come for me! You came back for me!"

Marlon began to sob. "I'm here, Pop. I've come to take you home. "He sniffed a little and wiped the tears from his eyes. 'It's good to see you. I missed you. I missed you!" They looked at each other, amazed to see how much they had evolved over time. Then they chuckled.

"I know you haven't heard me say this before…and I can't don't blame you. But I want you to know this: I love you. I'm very proud of you…of what you have become. You're a better man than I could have been, and I am happy that you've turned out better than I could have asked for. You're a hero."

Marlon looked at him, his palms resting on his father's shoulders. "That really means a lot coming from you. You are the hero. I'm just a kid who misses his father. All this time you've taught me the meaning of sacrifice, commitment, and forgiveness. Good or bad, you taught me how to be better man…to be a good soldier." The two embraced once more. "I'm gonna need to get us a couple of tickets so we can head back home. Take a seat, and I'll be right back with our tickets."

Eli sat down, as he held on to Marlon's forearm. "I need to tell you something."

Marlon stood still, curious to hear his father's words. "Sure, Pop. What is it?"

"My time here is short, son."

"Did you wait long?' Marlon asked. "I'm gonna get us a couple of tickets. Hopefully, we'll hop on the next train and head back. My pickup is parked at another terminal."

"No, no. That's not what I'm trying to say."

140

"You okay? You seem flushed," Marlon asked with a sobering tone.

"I feel great. Listen, my time is running out, and I'll be leaving soon."

"Ah, okay, Pops, but can you hang on while I grab an extra?" Marlon asked. "This won't take long. Just hang tight. Be right back. This shouldn't take long." He walked off hastily toward the ticket booth and stood behind two people waiting in line. 'Don't worry 'bout your stuff. I'll take it when I come back," he yelled.

As he waited, Eli sat back. He looked at his son, his face glowing as he reveled in the moment. Then his eyes shifted at the other end of the terminal. He gently rested his suitcase over his lap and straightened his fedora. Then he smiled, leaned back, and closed his eyes.

Marlon noticed his father sitting at the end of the pew with his head hung low and his shoulders hunched. He grinned slightly. *"Man's tired,"* he thought. Then he approached the ticket booth and purchased two one-way tickets back to Atlanta. He thanked the cashier, glanced at the time, then walked slowly back to his father. As he approached him, he noticed that he never moved. His posture appeared familiar. His head was down, and his shoulders sunken in. He stood in front of him, staring intently. He tapped his right shoulder. "Pop?"

Eli was unresponsive.

Marlon squeezed his right shoulder, but he remained still. Then he leaned closer and felt the side of his face. It was cold—he was lifeless. Marlon sobbed quietly. Then he stood up and took one step back. *"He's gone."*

As he stood there staring intently, several people came by and approached him then called for a paramedic. After several minutes, the paramedic arrived and tried to resuscitate the old man, but Eli was gone. Marlon remained quiet, staring at his father as the crowd quietly gathered around them.

The paramedic shook his head. "I'm sorry. He's gone."

Marlon kneeled down and kissed Eli on the forehead. "So long, Pop. It was a good life. I will see you when I can. Tell Mom...I said hi. I miss her," he whispered.

"There are a lot of people waiting for you," Sam said.

Eli felt the euphoria. A subtle feeling of peace and pure love surrounded him. His face appeared that of a man in his mid-thirties; the time where he found himself at the atrium of his life. He was young again, and he felt the vigor surging within him. The energy that once faded was renewed, and he felt healthier and flawless. He breathed a short sigh and smiled at the man standing next to him.

"I'm ready," he said.

"I'm glad to take you home, Eli," the man said.

Eli knew him. He's never met the man in the flesh, but deep down, he knew who he was. The man appeared in white robe with a golden sash around his waist. His hair was as white as snow, and his beard perfectly lining his jaw was as white as the hair that stretched down his neck.

"Do you think they'll recognize me?" Eli asked cheerfully.

"They know. She's waiting for you. I've been waiting for you. Welcome home," the man said.

"It's good to see you, Lord. I've waited my whole life. I've dreamt of this day."

"I know." He ushered him through the bright light as they faded to eternity.

Marlon glanced back and felt a strong presence behind him. "*I'll see you someday, Pops. I'll be all right.*" He walked over to the paramedics as they placed his father's body on the stretcher. "I'm coming with you," he said.

The people around him were shocked to see the whole incident unfolding. Many gave their condolences, then moved on. Strangers who witnessed Eli's passing felt slight sorrow—a somber reminder of losing a loved one, but for Marlon, it felt benign, a shallow gesture of sympathy offered without substance or meaning.

Chapter Fifteen

The next morning, Marlon awoke to the alarm clock set on the side of the bed of a dilapidated motel room. The dark, dingy motel room accommodated his melancholy. He slept through the night and awoke to the reality that his father was gone. All the emotions bottled inside him; the trauma from past combat experience, the difficult childhood, the failing marriage, the loss of his mother, and the struggle to cope from trauma swirled intensely within. His father's death brought the most painful past that grew lucid every ticking moment. The morose atmosphere ushered in the painful memories, pulling him back to the day when he stood by his mother's bedside, holding her by the hand as she drew her last breath.

Eight years had passed since his mother's death, but the memories remained vivid through the years. It was a clear, sunny day when he arrived at the airport from his first tour. The flight was physically draining, and his circadian rhythm was out of sync. He took a taxi from the airport to the hospital, toting his dusty army rucksack.

When he exited the unmarked taxi, the warmth embrace of the mild sunshine was invigorating, but the day was fraught with devastating news of his mother's decline. He felt homely, but out of place. She had reached the end of her days, fighting an incurable disease that left her gaunt and feeble.

She suffered through the agonizing brain tumor that ravaged her body for over a decade. Despite her deteriorating condition, she fought on for her husband and her two young boys, hoping to see them turn into the men she had longed for. The insidious disease had shut her body down and confined her under hospice care for many years (her benefactor was her former employer who willingly absorbed all the medical costs she incurred just to see her through). The family admired her deeply and made necessary concessions to sustain her health and see her through.

Marlon was granted a few days' leave from his tour in Iraq to tend to his dying mother, a short respite from his dangerous occupation. Returning home from the frontlines seemed tepid and inconvenient. It felt bittersweet-to leave the constant threat of death only to face a dying loved-one that led him to bouts of worry during the long flight. This homecoming turned tenuous when he arrived. He felt alone and dejected; being away from his men, and ignored by his family. But the short reprieve from constant threat buoyed his moodiness. His face was downcast as he entered the hospital, walking slowly through the empty hallway still dressed in his dingy battle uniform he had worn since his last patrol in Iraq.

The halls greeted him with the noxious stench of disinfectant mixed with antiseptic and human excrement lingering the air. Its narrow floors and its confining dark walls felt suffocating; the sound of the ticking clock and the endless sequential beeping machines annoyed him. As he came close to the door, he sensed a cloud of hopelessness penetrating the halls; it reminded him of the army field hospital where he came to identify and collect the tags of his fallen comrades.

He approached the reception desk. "Miss? Caroline Coe, where can I find her?" Without looking, the nurse pointed to the room a few doors down the hallway; her apathy was obvious and he grew indignant. He thanked her with sarcasm as he approached the room. He stood at the entrance where the door was shut. There were no names plates or names listed on the door except for three small digits plastered on it. He knocked gently on the door and hesitated before he opened it. He walked straight to her bedside without looking at his right or his left. She was fast asleep as he leaned closer to her.

He noticed his father slouching on the chair by the window. He was fast asleep. His brother was not present inside, and neither was his sister-in-law. Only the sound of the ventilation machine and the beeping heart monitor appeared lively. The room was musty and cold. It was the last room on the farthest end of the hospital, a section where the terminally ill were left ebbing away by the short-staffed hospital.

He gently placed his rucksack on this side of her bead, then he turned and looked at her without uttering a word, his face somber, his eyes glistened, and his eyelids were heavy. He noticed that her arms were pinned with IV needles. She wore a raggedy hospital gown that was two sizes larger. There was an oxygen line that ran up her nose over her crusted lips. Marlon grew pensive as he gazed at her wilting body that sunk on the flimsy mattress.

He was astonished to see the countenance of her face that emanated with such calm and unbridled peace. She was glowing—like a bride waiting on her wedding day. It was nothing short of extraordinary. He'd never seen anyone wear it with such grace; a subtle contradiction to his fractured pragmatism. He'd seen many of the soldiers suffer a tumultuous end; he has held the dying, those who struggled, gasping for every ounce of breath. The dying who clutched to every second of their life, desperately begging for reprieve from the inevitable unknown, fighting for every measure of time, begging to see the day unfold, hoping to unroll the night. Many good men had succumbed to their mortality under a misplaced, quixotic pretense. But Caroline defied this presumption, and she proved to him that he was unworthy to disrupt her peaceful slumber. He hesitated for a moment. Then gently eased his right hand under her fingers that rested by her side. He could feel her cold, stiff hand, and her shallow breathing leaving her nostrils. He slowly breathed a long sigh and inched closer. He felt the warmth of her breath gently touching his chin. He was consumed by her deteriorating condition; life was draining away from her, hastening her uneventful departure. She neither moved nor flinched as he gently caressed her forehead.

"Momma," he whispered. "It's me, Marlon." He smiled.

Still, there was no response. So he sat there and waited, hoping and wishing that she reciprocated. As he was about to move, he felt her fingers twitch. Then she heaved a long sigh, and gently opened her eyes. She looked at him with bewilderment, unable to recognize his face. After a long pause, her eyes widened.

"Baby?' she whispered with a course voice. "You…you made it back." She smiled, her eyes twinkled.

Marlon smiled and wiped the tears from his face. "You look great, Momma. You look really good."

"Baby, I'm a mess!" she replied with a jovial tone.

"Momma, don't be worried. You look…glorious." He grinned.

Eli awoke and sat up and gave Marlon a blank stare. He was still haggard and tired-reeling from the discomfort of the wooden chair. He had sat by her bedside for the past three days. He'd never seen his son for years, and Marlon's abrupt visit turned into an awkward encounter. But deep down, he was ecstatic and nervous to see his son, all grown up, brawny and rugged; his chiseled face and defined arms was a vision he never foresaw. It's been years since his son left for the military. Marlon left the house as a scrawny, timid teenager and returned as a gritty, self-made man; more than what his Eli could have expected. This was the same boy who constantly challenged him and tested his patience. Now, he appeared confident and imposing, a brooding man not easily aroused or sullied. He sat up and looked at his son, and they locked eyes. The two nodded in agreement without uttering a word.

"Baby?' his mother whispered. Her eyes were barely open, and her lips barely moved. 'I've missed you so much. I'm so happy you came back."

"I'm here, Momma. I am glad to see you. How are you holding up?"

"Oh, I'm feelin' dandy. Nothin' better. Jus' a bit of a headache is all." She smiled, but then she writhed in pain.

Elijah slowly stood up from his chair and walked toward the side of the bed. He looked at her, his eyes heavy and his face reeling from exhaustion. Then he winked at her, grinning slightly. He held her right hand. "Marlon is back, baby,' he said. Then he looked at Marlon. 'Good to see you son."

Marlon smiled then whispered, "Good to be back. Is there anything I can get you? Anything."

She smiled, gently shaking her head.

"Then what can I do? Is there anything I can do for you?"

She gestured for him to prop her up. He took several pillows from the closet and placed it under her neck. "Are you hungry? You thirsty?" he asked softly.

"I'm good, baby,' she replied with a coarse voice. "I'm just happy that you made it back. Will you be staying long?"

Marlon, sensing that she wanted to hear something positive, smiled in reply, "I dunno. It's really up to you. I can stay as long as you wanted me to. My commander wanted me to stay as long as I wanted to. But it's up to you," Marlon said.

She looked at her husband briefly, then her eyes wandered throughout the room. "Where…where is Charles?" she asked worriedly.

"Charles will not be here, baby. He's busy with church stuff," Eli replied.

"Oh…guess he betta' get to it then. I would have liked to have seen him," she said with deep longing.

"I'm pretty sure he'll be here to visit, Momma."

"Oh…I have no doubts. Now, come close and let me have a look at you." She squinted as she pulls him closer. Then she giggled. "Oh my, you have grown. Boy, you a grown man!" Marlon could feel her hollow laughter, as if her essence was ebbing away.

He glanced at Elijah. "Pops, what'd the doc say?"

Eli shook his head in grief. Marlon was distraught and began to sob.

"Oh, baby! Don't you cry for me. You best stop them tears. I ain't got the time to see you sad."

Marlon gently wiped his tears. "I…I'm scared for you," he said as he held on to her hand and gently caressed his jaw. "What's gonna happen to us?"

"You got nothin' to be scared of, baby. It's my time. God's callin' me home. My momma came to visit me in my dream. I'll be goin' home soon. But right now…" She looked deep into his eyes. "I'm just so happy I got to see you become the man I've long to see, that my eyes have seen the best things of this world. Tis been a while, and I missed you so much. Really glad that you made it home. Now, where's your brother?"

"He…he ain't here. Pops…well?" he looked at his father. Eli gently squeezed her shoulder.

"Charles will be here sometime soon, baby," Eli whispered.

"When?" she calmly asked.

"Soon…soon, baby," Eli answered.

"You need to lie down and rest before Charles gets here," Marlon prodded, easing her head down.

"Tell me, boy, did you find God while you were out there?"

"I…um, I'm not sure. Why'd you ask?"

"'Cause I've been prayin' for you, that you'll find what you need out there."

"I got everything that I need right here."

"Well, that's a good thing. I've been prayin' that God will protect you. Did you find him?"

Marlon shook his head. "I dunno, Momma, this is really not the time to talk about such thing."

"Boy, you need to find him. He's been waiting for you."

"I know. I know," he whispered.

"Find God, Marlon. He's waiting for you."

Marlon scoffed, "I think he's waiting for you."

She gently closed her eyes, easing herself comfortably as she writhed in pain. "I've been praying for you, baby. I hope that you will find God through this. Don't be angry. Be anxious for nothin'. Have faith. 'Cause God will see you through. Quit frettin' and start livin'. You are special, and you will change the world."

Marlon didn't utter any response. He simply laid her gently on her bed, making sure she was comfortable. He repeatedly stroked her frizzled, gray hair easing her back to sleep.

Several hours had passed, and Marlon and his father hardly parsed any lengthy words as he ambulated between the room and the nurse's station, anxiously checking, demanding to get hourly updates on her condition. That night, as the weather turned cold, the ominous clouds poured in a thunderstorm.

She was awakened by the sudden thunder striking near. As she awoke, she noticed Marlon looking at her, his eyes heavy, his jaws tight "You all right?" He cracked a smile.

"The loud bang startled me," she replied.

"Can I get you some water? Anything at all? Just nod if you are hungry," he asked with deep concern.

She pointed at Eli. "Wake your father up."

Marlon got up and went to his father who was fast asleep by the window. Neither the rain nor the loud thunder could disrupt him from his sleep.

"Pops!" Marlon shook him by the arm. "Pops!"

Eli was a bit shaken. "What is it?" He rubbed his eyes.

"Momma wants you."

"You all right, baby?" Eli asked as he got up, still haggard, dragging himself by her bedside.

"Baby, I'm sorry, but God is calling me home," she said.

Marlon quickly rushed out the door and called for the nurse to revive her.

Caroline smiled as she reached her hand up to the ceiling. "I see Momma holding her hand out to me. There's a man standing in front of her. He's holding his hand out and calling to me. He's glowing like the sun, but I can see his beautiful face."

"It's okay, Baby. Go to them," Eli whispered as he held her hand.

"Marlon, get Marlon here," she said.

Marlon came rushing through the door along with the tending nurse behind him. She quickly checked her wrist for her vital signs. The heart monitor was beeping more slowly.

Caroline noticed Marlon rushing through the door and by her side. He smiled at him. She held her hand out to him. "Take good care of your father. I will see you soon. I love you." Then she closed her eyes and drew her last breath.

Marlon, sensing that she was passing, quickly embraced her, her limbs sagged and her body lifeless. "No, no, no!' he cried. "No! No! Wait, Mom, the nurse is going to take care of you. Hang in there, okay?" The nurse pulled her away from him then tried to resuscitate her. "Momma! Hang in there, stay with me. Stay with me, doc's coming."

The doctor arrived and immediately took over and applied CPR. Once he found that she still couldn't revive her, he took the defibrillator and tried again to revive her. But her heart had flatlined too long; she was gone. He looked up the clock above her and declared her time of death. Then he took a step back and looked at Marlon.

"I'm sorry. But she's gone. There is nothing more we can do to bring her back," he said.

Marlon was incensed by the doctor's rapt remark. He wanted to hit him for such cold reply and apathy. But she was gone, and nothing could be done to revive her. Neither he nor his father responded. They just stood there holding her hand. The doctor and the nurse stepped outside and briefed the staff that the patient be relocated to the morgue to accommodate the incoming patient.

After a several minutes, after his tears had dried up, he leaned down and kissed her gently on the forehead. Then he looked at his father, his eyes appeared hazed, unable to piece the whole thing together. Eli couldn't find the words to console him. He had a glazed look, unable to fathom her passing.

Marlon was angered by his father's reaction. He pinned the blame on him for lack of urgency. Marlon stood up and backed away. "Send me the address of her grave. I'll visit her when I return," he said in a cold, stoic tone.

"Wha…wait, where you goin'?" his father asked.

"I'm headin' back to base. I'll be flying tomorrow back to Iraq."

As Marlon was about to step out of the room, Eli stopped him. "Um, wait a minute, son." He waived to him. "Why don't you stay? Pay respects and see your brother."

"I paid my share of respect. There's nothing for me here. I'm not staying. I've got a job to do. You and Charles…you can go and bury her. I can't go. I've got a job to do. It's too much!" He walked out the door. That following day, he was back in Iraq, walking the streets of Ramadi alongside his men.

The pain of losing his mother was unbearable. And being with his men, the men whom he trusted, and the ones who understood him—they were his place of solitude. Neither his faith nor his own family consoled him and alleviated the weight of grief. For ten years, he shunned his own family. The resentment he carried since childhood had calcified, and he had grown resentful of them, more so with his own father. There was no other place that he could find to lay down his own demons. He easily pinned his resentments on his own father. The guilt that he absorbed from his mother's death inflamed painful memories he harbored and carried through the battlefield. The repressed painful past fueled his rage—an emotion that he easily channeled against physical threats. These spurts of rage were heightened through fear and anxiety fighting the shadowy adversary relentlessly haunting him. He was angry and bitter. Not even his wife or his daughter could have redeemed him.

Only by divine intervention and the death of his father reignited the pain he suppressed for many years. But the grief brought closure; it brought down the walls and gave him some semblance of peace. The pain died with the loss of his loved ones. The serendipitous encounter opened his eyes, engulfing the spiritual void, and brought him to the altar of peace. He felt the weight lifted despite all the pain he endured. The resentment that haunted him had dissipated upon the last embrace. And the painful memories that confined him were finally lifted that fateful night.

He kept staring at the old, worn-out leather suitcase. He never opened it, but his curiosity grew fervently the longer he stared. After several hours, he decided to open it.

The suitcase felt lighter than he'd anticipated. To think that his father would have brought a heavier load to move in with him seemed out of place. He placed it over the bed and proceeded to open it. Much to his surprise, there were only two items that he found inside the case—an old picture of him and his brother during their teenage years and a small journal from his late mother.

The picture was meant to remind Eli of Marlon's face. The journal kept him occupied, a token of the past that he once cherished. *"Why would a man bring two things, no clothes, no money, no paper-nothing,"* he thought. But he soon realized that his father did not bring this for himself, but rather for his son; to find restitution for past mistakes and to reconnect with his estranged brother. These two items stirred up all the emotions he's bottled inside, and it brought him to tears. Without hesitation, he took out his cell phone, wiped the tears from his face and proceeded to make a call.

He flipped his phone open, scrolled down his contact list, and called the number. The phone rang several times, and Darcy answered, "Hello?"

"Darcy, this is Marlon," he calmly said.

"Hi, Marlon, how are things?" she asked. "Did you get to pick up your father?"

"Yes. Is…is Charles home?"

"Yes, hold on." She took the phone up to him. Charles was sitting outside on the back patio, sipping his coffee, watching his children play on the grass. "Charles, it's your brother." She handed the phone over.

Charles looked annoyed. "Marlon, did you get Dad?" he asked abruptly without any greeting.

"Pop's dead," Marlon replied.

There was silence on the line for almost a minute.

"Excuse me?" Charles asserted.

"He's gone, Charles."

Then Charles began sobbing quietly.

Charles cleared his throat. "What happened? Was there an accident?"

"No! Listen, it was no accident." Marlon stood up from his bed. "Just his time, Charles."

"When?" he asked, his voice quivered.

"Last night. When I got to the terminal, he was fine. He…he was… happy," Marlon replied softly.

"I'm coming to take him," Charles asserted.

"Listen, Pops would not have it any other way. He wanted to see Mom, and it was just his time."

Charles choked up a bit. "I should have just kept him here. This would have been averted."

"Pop's dead, Charles. There's nothing else we can do. I will take him back with me and bury him next to Mom in Georgia. I have to make some phone calls. Listen, I will call you for the funeral arrangements." Marlon paused. "I have to go." He ended the call.

Charles's children heard their father sobbing. They came and stood by him, wondering why their father wore a somber face. Charles looked at his two kids, then he knelt down, then quietly embraced them.

"What's wrong, Daddy?" his son asked, but Charles did not answer.

Darcy appeared from the patio door and began to weep. She heard the conversation behind the screened porch. Then she approached him, kneeled down, and embraced him tightly. No words were enough to comfort him as he grew hysterical, sobbing on her bosom. They remained there for quite some time until their eyes were dry.

Marlon looked at his phone and searched for the phone number he needed. When he found it, he hesitated. Then the phone rang. It was a new number. Again, he hesitated. But he knew that the call was important.

"Hello," Marlon answered.

"Captain Marlon Coe," the caller responded.

"Yes?"

"It's Major Wellis. US Army Judge Advocate General"

"Sir!"

"I hope that I didn't disturb you."

"No, no, you're fine." He paused. "What can I help you with, Major?"

"You and Colonel Darak spoke of your impending trial, and I wanted to reach out to you on the status of the case. We need to discuss your trial."

He breathed a deep sigh. "Sure, let's hear it." He sat up, anxiously awaiting his fate.

"The brass reviewed the case and, they deemed you fit for trial. Article 92 of the UCMJ."

Marlon sighed. "Accessory to murder, and…Deriliction of duty? But, why?"

"I'm afraid so. That was what was decided by brass. It is highly politicized.' Wellis sighed. "You knew this was coming."

Marlon scoffed. "When and where, sir?"

"Two weeks tops. I'll send you the details."

"Thank you, sir." Marlon ended the call.

He waited for several minutes thinking of his upcoming trial. Then he scrolled through his contact list and found the number he hoped was missing. He pushed the call button and waited. After four rings, he decided to hang up. Just before he ended the call, a soft, little voice came on the other end.

"Hello?" the little voice answered.

Marlon leaned closer and smiled "Hello?" she asked again.

"Ensleigh?"

"Who's this?" She asserted with a distinct, adorable lisp.

Marlon was awestruck. He paused momentarily, and then he began sobbing. Ensleigh heard him sobbing over the phone.

"Are you okay?" she asked gently. But Marlon couldn't restrain himself. And just before he spoke, someone took the phone from her.

"Hello?" Cheryl asked.

Marlon wiped his tears away with his knuckles, then cleared his throat. "Cheryl," he uttered softly.

There was silence. Marlon waited for her answer, expecting an immediate reply, but she remained quiet.

"Cheryl, it's me."

"It's…It's been a while," she replied.

"I know…I'm sorry."

"Are you okay?' she asked. 'Is everything all right?"

"My dad passed away last night."

"I…I'm sorry." She hesitated for a moment then began to sob. "What happened?"

"It was just his time. He died peacefully."

"And how are you holding up?"

"I'll get by. It's just the way it's supposed to be."

"How can we help?"

"Umm, I dunno. Thought I'd let you know," he said. Then Marlon turned aloof.

"I…I gotta go." He hung up the phone without saying good-bye, cutting the call short. He readied himself to leave. He stepped outside the motel room half an hour later and walked across the street to tend to retrieve his father.

"Ashes to ashes, dust to dust. Naked am I when I came, and naked will I when return to the soil. In the name of the Father, Son, and the Holy Spirit, amen." the priest concluded as the undertakers lowered the coffin beneath the wet grassy knoll.

Eli's sons, along with their wives and children, gathered around his coffin. Each one wore a somber face, quietly sobbing. Only the priest, the two undertakers, and the family stood under the clear sky, looking straight down as the coffin was lowered.

Marlon bent and took a fistful of dirt and tossed it over the coffin. When he stood up and turned, his brother embraced him. Then Charles kneeled down and grabbed a handful of dirt and poured it over his father's coffin. Then the rest of the family, including the children, tossed a pink rose over the coffin.

After a brief silence, they left the grave and headed back home. But Marlon went his way. As he began to leave, Cheryl quietly and softly took his hand and smiled. "We'll be here when you're ready to come home."

He looked at her, and slightly nodded his head. Then he walked on and drove off without looking back. He neither turned to the right or the left.

Chapter Sixteen

He glanced down on his wristwatch. It was four o'clock in the afternoon. An hour of ceaseless verbal exchange between his lawyer had passed. Major Wellis was relentless, badgering the key witness on the stand. Sergeant Framm made no concession as Wellis crossed-examined him, detailing every question raptly, parsing the lawyer's statements to discredit his claims. Framm remained obstinate and resolute, proclaiming his innocence due to mental lapses. He laid all the blame on his commanding officer on that fateful day when the team lost nine men from the attack.

"This trial is taking too long, he thought. *I can't keep up with this lowlife. I just want this to be over with."* He kept his eyes fixated on Framm to show the judges that he was not to be intimidated; Framm's demeanor gave no hint of remorse or guilt to their inquisitive stare.

"The captain ordered you to lay suppressive fire, did he not?" Major Wellis asked.

"Yes, sir, he did," Framm asserted.

"Then why did you not follow his orders, Sergeant? If there's someone guilty of article 15, it should be the platoon sergeant."

"I disagree, sir."

"You disagree!" Wellis patronized him.

"Yes, sir! I gave orders to the men to regroup, but it was almost too late. We were caught in a crossfire, and the captain was in no condition to make rash, sound decisions for the safety of the team and for retreat."

"So, enlighten me. What do you think Captain Coe should have done?"

"Well, sir, military SOP dictates that the commanding officer is to assess the battle and engage the enemy and retreat to safety to regroup.'

Framm paused and looked at the judges. "He clearly violated that. For that reason, more men died because of this decision."

"The decision to stay put?"

"That's correct, sir!" Framm asserted.

"Wait! Isn't it part of military ethos to leave no a man behind?"

"It is, sir."

"Then if someone is guilty, shouldn't it be the platoon sergeant?"

"No, sir! The responsibility lies on the company commander. He was combat ineffective. We were caught in a vice, facing overwhelming numbers firing from three sides at higher elevation. And we were not in a position to fight. We needed to take cover, and the captain refused to do that."

"Did you follow his orders, Sergeant?"

"I…tried, sir."

"What do you mean you tried? Did you or did you not follow his orders?"

"I…I don't recall him giving me specific orders."

"Well, so you didn't follow orders?' Wellis turned to the three judges on the panel. 'You didn't follow orders, because you didn't know what he said, did you?"

Framm squirmed slowly and cleared his throat. "No, sir!"

Wellis approached him closer. "I'm sorry, Sergeant. The judges didn't hear you. Repeat your statement."

Framm straightened his shoulders and blurted. "No, sir!"

"You know what the captain said to you? What he ordered you to do?' Wellis paused. 'He ordered you to lay suppressive fire and find cover behind the houses closer to the mountains while you wait for artillery and air support.' He turned to the jury.

'Sound military doctrine dictates that when engaged in an ambush, that overwhelming firepower is the best course of action to engage head-on and disrupt enemy initiative. Retreat was never mentioned in the army manual. Captain Coe was warned that there were enemy combatants in the vicinity, and that's what he was ordered to do… to capture or kill a high-value target, gather Intel, assess enemy force capacity, and if necessary, engage and destroy. He was not ordered to retreat but ordered to wait. And that's what he did. He followed orders that led to mounting casualties."

The jury remained quiet.

"Tell me, Sergeant, is that the reason why you left your post that night…to return the favor?" Wellis asked.

"I…was told that the Taliban would be there and stay at the village. It was dark. I couldn't understand what they said. But they wanted me dead, so I killed them…as ordered to kill the enemy."

"The enemy, Sergeant? What enemy?"

"They were there inside the village. They were waiting for me. But I got there first."

"Is that the reason, Sergeant? Is that your reason to kill fifteen innocent civilians? Where were their weapons? Did they fire at you?"

"It was dark. I got clumsy."

"Clumsy!" Wellis screamed. "They were families, Sergeant! All of them…children, parents, and the elderly. You killed them all! You massacred those families with reckless abandonment!"

Framm was infuriated. "I disagree, sir! They were enemy combatant. If not, then they were guilty for abetting the enemy."

Wellis looked straight at the judges. "Why did you do it, Sergeant?"

Framm refused to relent and began yelling. "Sir, I was told that we were going to conduct a nighttime assault on the Taliban that night. They should be on this chair. Marlon should be in this chair, not me!"

"And you decided to go on your own, leave the base and deliver justice. Outside military of protocols, without notifying your superiors, or asking for permission, did you? You went into the village and murdered fifteen innocent men, women, and children. Is that it?"

The senior defense attorney stood up. "Objection! Leading the witness."

"Overruled, until the defendant is proven innocent, he is considered as such by military tribunal,' the senior judge replied calmly. 'Please, continue, Major Wellis."

Wellis walked in front of Framm. "You killed those people, and you're blaming your commanding officer," he whispered.

"It was his fault, his incompetence that got so many the men killed, including First Sergeant Miller!" Framm bellowed.

"You're pinning the blame and the blood of those people for your commanding officer's decision. Their blood is in your hands, Sergeant! Captain Coe did what was best under the circumstance, and you took matters into your own rifle, then shot and killed innocent civilians in the middle of the night!' Wellis walked back behind the table and turned around. 'No further questions, your Honors." He sat down and looked at his notes The senior judge pounded the gavel. "Thank you, Major. Does the defense want to continue?" the judge asked.

Major Wellis and Marlon stood up. "No further questions at this time, sir," Wellis replied.

The senior judge nodded. "Thank you, Sergeant Framm, you may return to your seat."

Framm nodded then proceeded to leave the courtroom being escorted by two military policemen. Marlon looked him in the eyes without flinching. Framm reciprocated with disdain as he walked passed him, his class A army uniform sagged over his tall, lanky frame. Marlon kept his eyes on him until Framm sat down behind the bar.

Wellis stood up behind the defendant's table. "Sir, I have one more witness ready to take the stand."

Marlon stood up erect, then paced himself to the stand. He raised his right hand and swore an oath. He quickly sat down, eager to field any questions.

"Captain, you've heard all the testimonies of the men under your command that fateful day. Please give us a complete account of what happened that day?" Wellis asked.

"Yes, sir,' he replied. 'We were tasked to ascertain enemy troop movement within and around the village. Soft intel reported that at least two hundred to four hundred Taliban and Al-Qaeda fighters converged on our vicinity, preparing to assault the base. We had good indication of this due to prior engagements and random mortar fire from the hills in and around our base the previous nights.

"We needed to check the village to see if they were harboring any enemy combatants, weapons, and contrabands detrimental to the progress of rebuilding it. We needed to engage the enemy head-on to determine its size, capacity, equipment, and tactical mission. I was ordered find, capture, or kill a high-ranking officer hiding inside the village. I was also ordered to meet with the elders and calm the populace, but it seemed that the Taliban were waiting for us to enter and engage us from the hilltop to the west. Needless to say, we were caught off guard. The Taliban, as we have found, were moving weapons and ammo the previous day, hoping to lure us into a trap. We had faulty intel. The intel given to us from unnamed sources was a day late. And we paid dearly for it.' Marlon's eyes started to glisten as tears rolled down his face. "We lost nine men that day," he added as the courtroom gasped.

"Did you execute your orders, Captain?" Wellis asked.

"Yes, as I was directed by Colonel Moreo," he replied calmly. Marlon gave his testimony, every detail of the account at Wanat from the beginning to the time of rescue. His testimony reached its finality when he gave account of his orders to hold ground half an hour into the firefight.

"You ordered your men to continue and repel enemy attack. Why?" Wellis asserted.

"We simply could not abandon our position due to the men that we've lost from the explosion. It was imperative. I made the critical decision not to leave First Sergeant Miller and Khaled and the rest of my dead buddies to the Taliban. We never, never leave our fallen behind!"

"Did you call for immediate extraction?"

"We were promised air support, but air support never came during intense firefight. They arrived after nine men were killed during the firefight. Senior command deemed it unnecessary and dangerous to send in air support, fearing civilian casualties and poor weather conditions. Medevac was delayed due to the enemy's position on high ground. Artillery was the only immediate support I received to keep the enemy from overrunning our perimeter. My gunner was the only one who kept them pinned down until he ran out of ammo and was killed."

"If you felt that you were out-gunned, why did you not retreat?"

"Retreat was a viable option. And it may have saved more lives, that I don't know. But given the circumstances, and the incoming artillery, I decided to stay put until it was safe to leave. Unfortunately, it came too late. By that time, many guys in my team had been injured and killed in action. Would the retreat earlier have saved more lives? I honestly don't know. But we're Green Beret's, we never back away from a fight. We complete our mission. That's what we're trained to do. We don't back down. We fight until we win!" Marlon asserted.

"Thank you, Captain. No further questions." Wellis sat back down.

"Does the prosecution want to cross-examine the defendant?" the judge asked.

The defense attorney stood up. "We do, sirs." He approached Marlon. "Captain Coe, you said that command informed you earlier that there were an army of two hundred to four hundred enemy combatants around the village. But you proceeded to the village despite this. Why?"

"Our mission was to capture or kill a high value target, sir."

"Were you not aware that they were waiting for you?" the prosecutor asked.

"We had a good idea that an ambush was likely. That's why I radioed in for air support and eyes on the sky in case the enemy decides to engage us."

"Yet you continued and delayed your stay. Earlier, you noted that you wanted to talk to the villagers, which caused further delays that placed your team inside the enemy's crosshairs. You lingered on." He pointed at Marlon.

"That's our secondary mission, sir."

"Did you not see this Captain? It's written all over the map. You ignored the soft intel and proceeded to go and you lingered in one place."

"We did not waste any time, sir. And based on that same Intel, we had the opportunity to kill a high value target. And that's why our defensive perimeter was not completely set at an optimum simply because we did not want to anger the villagers."

"Is it possible, Captain Coe that you hastily assembled your team and neglected protocols to take a larger force, return to base immediately, and call for extraction at a secondary point? To prepare for any possible enemy engagements?" he asked sarcastically.

"Anything is possible, sir. We just can't tell when and where the enemy would come from."

"But you were warned, Captain."

"I was informed, sir. I was not warned. The lack of Intel made it difficult to ascertain enemy numbers and position. That's the fog of war."

"So, not only were you informed of potential larger enemy force, but your platoon sergeant gave you the initiative to retreat out of range, did he not?"

"The sergeant's role is to execute my orders, sir. He's not in a position to give orders for retreat unless I am incapable of command," he replied petulantly.

"You chose to stay, and for that, you incurred further casualties, jeopardizing the lives of you and your men, rather than take necessary steps to disengage and retreat. You wanted to pick a fight, and you got it…at the expense of your team."

"Sir, I don't know why or what my orders have anything to do with Framm's abhorrent retribution."

"Indulge me, Captain. Did you listen to Sergeant Framm's input?"

Marlon cleared his throat. "I have never been in a position where my conduct led to the detriment of my team. I've made the call, I bore the responsibility, and we were caught in a vice. No one…not one could have seen it coming. Not I, not Sergeant Framm, not the intel, not the villagers. The only man I know that could have foreseen the whole thing was the man who stood on the middle of the road holding his burro. Only God himself could have seen this coming. Those men died because of what we didn't know. Despite of the outcome, these men gave their full measure." He stopped and looked Framm in the eyes. "I led my team as ordered. We executed the mission as planned. We incurred casualties. We stood our ground. That's the Green Beret. We don't back away from a fight! Like everyone else who signed up for this, Sua Sponte"

"Is it pride, Captain? Is it the thought of losing that made you stay? Is it the failure that you're afraid of? Or is it plain complacency?"

"Sir, if I was afraid, I sure wouldn't be here. Yes, I was scared. We all were! Pride?" He scoffed. "That's what kept us on our feet. We fail when we live to see another day, when few of us remain standing next to the coffin of our buddies heading home to their widows and orphans. I stood by our credo, and we lost men…good men like Robben, Percy, Yrata, Gronn, Martins, Brown, Khal, Trujillo, and First Sergeant Miller. We lost that day not because of my decision. We lost because our buddies died. And…if there's someone to blame, I'll take the blame. I am responsible. But I was not complicit, nor do I condone Framm's retribution!"

"Those men died under your watch and Framm reacted based on your actions and inaction."

"They died for something they believed in. Framm fought for something he believed in. The difference between us and him is that he believed in a twisted, evil form of justice that none of us, neither Miller nor anyone else on my team would have fought for. We came to build up. He came to tear down.

"Thank you, Captain." The prosecutor interrupted. "No further questions, sirs."

"Captain Coe, you may return to your seat," the senior judge ordered.

"Permission to be dismissed, sir?"

"Granted."

The judge ordered the court to stand. "Do you have any further witnesses, Major?" the judge asked.

"We will take an hour recess and return at fifteen hundred hours. Court is adjourned."

The court recessed for deliberation. Later that afternoon, Marlon awaited his fate. Sitting on the bench, he leaned against the white marble wall, looking at the empty hall and its polished floors; his eyelids were heavy, as he fielded a blank stare. He leaned his head against the marble wall then closed his eyes and fell asleep. The mental fatigue brought him nearly into a catatonic state and opened the door to the past gushing with painful memories that is vividly portrayed.

"Sergeant!' he yelled. 'Get the men on the mortars and give me covering fire on that hill. Secure the perimeter and get me some snipers on the rooftops for cover. Relay all enemy location."

"Sir, we're out in the open. We're sitting ducks!"

"Get the men behind the walls, Sergeant." He took the C-B radio and rushed inside one the houses followed by the rest of squad.

"Echo Two-Four Alpha, this is Whiskey Five-Six. Over! Echo Two-Four Alpha...this is Whiskey Five-Six. Over!" His voice was hurried and loud.

"This is Echo Two-Four Alpha. Reading you loud and clear, Whiskey Five-Six. What's your stat?"

"Two KIA. Four wounded. Still combat effective, over! Combat effective!" he shouted. "ETA on the bird?"

The radio crackled, "Helo in-bound two mikes."

Marlon looked at his men waiting for orders. "We've got Apache inbound, two mikes."

He breathed a long sigh of relief as the rhythmic chopping sound of the Apache grew louder. Within minutes, the Apache gunship indiscriminately strafed the hillside where the enemy was entrenched. When the gunships left, the artillery fire began pounding the hillside for half an hour.

Marlon and his men huddled inside several houses, waiting artillery to subside. As the howitzers intensified, Marlon and the rest of his team hastily retreated back to base to avoid the Taliban fighters pressing their assault downhill. The deafening, bombardment maimed and killed anyone at the hilltop while Marlon's team pinned anyone out in the open with intense cover fire.

After the cannons had ceased, nothing was left except for large craters strewn with dead or dying enemy fighters. The rest of them hastily fled further uphill to avoid getting caught in the open by the snipers. When the firefight ended, the hilltop became eerily quiet as the Taliban and Al-Qaeda fighters were in full retreat.

Sensing that the enemy may have fled, Marlon immediately ordered the wounded to be medevacked to the nearest base. He and his men quickly mounted the Humvees and fled the village to avoid incurring more casualties.

Chapter Seventeen

He hadn't left the seat since the court adjourned. He was growing anxious as the judges' deliberation dragged through the entire afternoon. At four o'clock, Major Wellis returned from the courtroom. When he saw him, he stood at attention.

"They're ready for you," Wellis said.

Marlon gave a salute, slightly unusual for a soldier to salute a superior officer inside the building. "Sir! Whatever the outcome, I just want to thank you for fighting on my behalf."

"My brother would have followed you through the gates of hell. Everything he said about you is true. You're a good leader. I don't know how things unraveled during firefights, but you made the right choice, and your men respect you for that. Captain, I've done what I could to return you to your men." Wellis opened the door to the courtroom, and ushered him in. "I'm sure that it wouldn't be long that you will be deployed again."

Marlon smiled. "For what it's worth, all that I've given, all that I've done, I followed orders. I completed the mission, and my men and I fought for each other," he whispered.

Wellis nodded, his brow wrinkled. "Let's go."

After four hours of deliberation, the three judges issued a verdict. Each gave a summary each witness's testimonies of their account in Wanat, scrutinizing every piece of evidence applicable within the Uniform Code of Military Justice—whether the commanding officer acted in accordance to military battlefield manual.

Marlon faced trial for dereliction of duty that led to the death of nine men and his complicit involvement in the massacre of fifteen civilian

Afghanis. Should he be found guilty of blatant violation of article 92 or any hint of callousness be warranted, he will face imprisonment. Framm's testimony was more pronounced in the eyes of the judges. The senior JAG officer called Marlon to stand as he deliberated the verdict.

"Captain Marlon James Coe you have been charged with failure to obey order regulation of the US military code in direct violation of article 92-B-3A and 92-B-3B under the Uniform Code of Military Justice. You are also charged of complicit involvement for the death of fifteen innocent civilians on the Fifteenth of July 2008. All testimonies have been reviewed and all witnesses accounted for." The senior JAG paused and looked at Marlon. 'All three judge advocate generals have found you not guilty of violation of the article 92-B-3A and 92-B-3B. Both counts will be expunged from your service record. In violation of article 120 of the Uniform Code of Military Justice, you are hereby guilty of the charge. You will be stripped of your rank and relieved of command. Your service will be terminated under dishonorable discharge."

Marlon stood quietly; his chin raised and his shoulders cocked. As he listened to the verdict, he didn't display any reaction. He was angry and defiant, but he made no gesture nor reacted unkindly. He was fully aware of the ramifications of being found guilty of the lesser charge. His steely, empty gaze gave no hint of chagrin or excitement. He simply took the verdict as it was delivered.

"The defendant is found not guilty of any charges, nor is he complicit of Sergeant Framm's atrocities."

Marlon closed his eyes and gently breathed a long sigh of relief. The senior judge proceeded to complete his delivery. "However, due to the extenuating circumstances, the death of nine service members under your command and the death of innocent civilians from the hands of one of your noncommissioned officers, have led us to discharge you from your post and from the US Army." Marlon hung his head. "This verdict is final, and the defendant will be removed from his post. He will be discharged dishonorably from the service. His rank and pay will be stripped effective immediately." The senior judge went on. 'Captain Marlon Coe your service is hereby terminated effective immediately. You are relieved of your duties from the US Army."

Marlon looked at each of the judges, and he stood motionless. He was in total shock of the verdict. He had not expected to be dishonorably discharged, which was the last thing on his mind. But there was nothing he could do. The verdict was handed with complete prejudice.

"Do you have any last statement before the court is dismissed?" the judge asked.

"Sir, no, sir!"

"Very well." The judge lifted his gavel.

But before he dropped the gavel, Marlon interrupted. "There is one thing that I would like to say," he blurted.

The judges looked at each other, and the senior judge nodded. "You may proceed."

"I served my life in this outfit. I am one of the lucky few. My men and I gave it our all and many had fallen. All of us gave some, and some of us gave all. I did what I could under the circumstances, and if…if I had to relive the past, I wouldn't have done anything differently. I was trained to follow orders. We lived out our credo, that no warrior is left behind, no matter what the cost. My men and I did that, and they would have done the same for me, for you, and for each man who bore that flag. I am responsible for my men and the lives that were lost. Like my predecessors, I bartered the lives of so many good men, men that are worth ten civilians, for some piece of land that grows nothing but opium. They died because I made those decisions as I was trained to do so, and I accept my fate. I just ask that my honor be restored and my name be exonerated from guilt. If nothing else would convince you, please do not ignore the years of my service." Marlon was choked up.

The judges remained silent, and the gavel fell without reciprocity for his plea.

The audience remained silent as he resigned to his seat. He hung his head and sobbed quietly. Major Wellis stood next to him, and patted his shoulder, a kind but shallow gesture. Then he stepped away without uttering any solemn word.

Marlon sat there until the courtroom was empty. Slowly, he took a small pin from his lapel and placed it over the table. He stood up, straightened his uniform, and walked out of the courtroom. He slowly eased his beret over his head as he headed outside.

No one was present outside to greet him; no one gave any heed or accolades at the front steps. He stopped and looked around to see if there were anyone waiting to ask him of the verdict, but the trial went unnoticed. As he walked to his car parked in an open lot, he noticed a woman standing by the lamppost. She was holding a young boy in her arms.

He looked at her as he came close. She immediately approached him as he was about to enter his truck.

"Excuse me. Captain Marlon Coe?" the woman asked courteously. Marlon gazed at her curiously.

"Can I help you, ma'am?"

"I'm Diane Miller, Sergeant Miller's wife," she uttered as she took a step closer. "I wanted to meet you, and I found out."

Marlon was quite surprised. "Mrs. Miller," he leaned closer. He was ashamed of the verdict that may have reached her. "I'm really sorry… about your husband."

She was slightly awkward and shy.

"I…uh, I wanted to thank you for coming, but you missed the verdict," he answered timidly.

"That's not why I came. I wanted to let you know." She glanced at the boy clinging to her side. "My son and I wanted to tell you that you did the right thing."

Marlon blew a shallow breath and embraced her. "No one has ever told me that until now. It's been a while, and to hear it from you means many things," he whispered, his voice cracking.

She quietly reciprocated the embrace and stepped back shortly thereafter. "I want you to meet Caleb. This is Sam's son. He's the only child we had." She smiled as tears rolled down her right eye.

He smiled. "Hey there, buddy. So, you're the one that kept your father grounded, huh?" He patted his blondish head. "How old is he?"

"He's about to turn one." She smiled.

Marlon tilted his head, he was slightly curious. "He was born before your husband's death?" She nodded. "I'm truly sorry," he added.

"Oh, don't be," he said slightly grinning. "Sam didn't tell you?"

"No. He never mentioned it to me. I wish he did."

"Well, that's Sam. He's very private. Doesn't really like to share things, even to his buddies. It's hard enough for me to ask him what he did in Afghanistan."

Marlon smirked. "Yeah, that's Sam all right." He paused for a bit as the boy started to whimper.

"Um, how are you doing? How is he doing?"

"Caleb is good. He's a good boy. Takes after his father's energy. He definitely has his bravery patted down." She laughed.

Marlon chuckled and paused, feeling a bit awkward. Then he looks her in the eyes. "Is there anything I can do?"

"Actually, I came here to see you. I'm not here to ask for any favors. Sam took care of all of that, knowing that he may never come back to me. I came because I wanted to tell you that Caleb and I are fine, that Sam would have been proud of you. Sam knew what he signed up for. It was hard to accept it right after he left, but looking at the past and feeling regret and guilt doesn't make things easier. It won't bring him back. No one can bring him back to me. One of these days, I will come to him, but he will never come to me. This is the choice we make, and we just need to move on, day by day, until it doesn't feel so bad anymore. My son needs me, and I must move on. I have to be there for him."

Marlon paused a bit and pondered as he gazed on the boy's eyes. "Is there anything…anything that I can do for you?"

She began sobbing. "Caleb and I will manage. But if there's one thing that I want to ask…is that when my son gets to be older, you'll visit him and tell him stories about his father. I want my son to know his father and you were there right beside him when he was out of my reach. If there's something you can do, that's all Sam would have asked from you."

Marlon took one of the pins from his lapel, a small, shiny Army Special Forces tab from his left pocket. "This is my gift to your son, that he'll remember me and his father, and when he turns twelve, I will tell him what his father did…when he's ready.'

He took out a piece of paper and scribbled his address and phone number. Then he handed it to her and embraced her. "Anything you need, anything at all, I'll be a phone call away." He gently ran his fingers on the boy's wavy hair and smiled. He bid them farewell, then walked back to his vehicle.

As he entered his truck she walked right up by his window. "My husband…told me to tell you that you were a good leader. He loved serving his country under your command. He was very proud of what you've done to lead the team, and he would have been proud of you standing up to do the right thing. You couldn't bring him back, but you and your men brought him back home to me. I'm sure that God has called you for a greater purpose,' She sobbed. 'He won't come to me, but he is with us."

Marlon looked at her and looked at the boy. "Ya know, since he died, I could never remember the sound of his voice. I could hardly remember his face until I look at your son." Then he smiled and drove off.

That night, after a quiet and long cogitation, as he sat on his worn out sofa, he started noticing the things that pervaded his purview. Every part of the room was lit brightly, revealing cherished items that once proved useful; books, toys, and small souvenirs from his wife and child, things he had forgotten.

Then something caught his eyes -the photos resting over the mantle. He stood up and held one picture closer, and he began to smile. It was a photo of him and all his men who served in his company, each man wearing his combat gear under the bright sun. Everyone appeared jovial and laid back. "*Good men!*" he thought. Then he pulled the picture out and slid it on his back-pocket.

He unbuttoned his class A uniform and hung it over the chair. Then he took his green beret and rested it on the seat. He untied his shoes slowly and slid off his trousers. Then he walked on to the closet on his underwear and grabbed pair of worn out blue jeans and a white buttoned shirt. He took his pistol, which rested on the nightstand. He unloaded the magazine and popped the bullet from the barrel. He tossed the pistol over the bed along with the magazine. "*If this is the only way, then I lived for nothing,*" he thought.

As he glanced around, he stumbled on the open magazines lying over the coffee table, its edges worn with its faded satin cover. Its illustrations were wrinkled and dusty. "Time to turn the page," he mumbled.

He grabbed his keychain on the counter and unlatched the key to his truck from its keychain. He tossed the rest of the keys to the table. Then he proceeded to exit the apartment. He switched the lights off. He glanced at the room for the last time. "Never again...not coming back!" he whispered. He smiled then gently closed the door.

Chapter Eighteen

That dreary Sunday morning brought in fewer parishioners to the early service. Charles was mulling over his sermons, his notes randomly strewn over his desk. It's been a few weeks since his father's burial, and he was unprepared. The grief took longer than he had expected.

He glanced at his wristwatch and noticed that the service was about to start within a minute. *"It's nine o'clock. There's no more time. I can stay here forever, waste away, or I can do what I could be good at,"* he thought as he hastily piled up his notes.

He briskly walked over from the back of the church over to the front of the pew where he usually sat every Sunday. He noticed everyone looking at him as he sat down next to his wife and two children.

Darcy was a bit shocked of his blatant tardiness. The children were still a bit groggy as they rushed to the church. Nevertheless, they sat quietly as expected while they waited for their father to begin. Not many parishioners appeared enthused on that typical early service. While some arrived early, those who were tardy were quietly ushered by the elders to the front pew where seats appeared vacated-a subtle act of chastisement.

Without delay, an old woman led the congregation to an old hymn, pressing her fragile fingers gently on the weathered ivory keys. The people reciprocated kindly to her slow, arrhythmic song.

Charles kept his eyes at his family. As he stood up to begin his sermon, he noticed the doors slightly open. There appeared his brother, sneaking in to attend the service. Marlon went in and sat on the last row, slowly squeezing his way through a crowded back pew. Charles grinned slightly as he opened his Bible. He was excited to see his brother's unexpected arrival; it felt like homecoming on a Christmas day. He was invigorated by his brother's unannounced visit. Then he looked down and read verses from the book of Jeremiah.

"Your old self has to die to give birth to a new life with renewed sense of vigor. A life destined for greater purpose, so that the lost will know that God can raise the dead to life!" Charles said enthusiastically. He went on and gave a short, but poignant speech directed at his parishioners fighting through their grogginess.

"Don't try to understand. Don't try to rationalize. Just go through it, every bit of the suffering. Take the hit and stand up to it. But you must remain faithful.' He added. Then he took a deep breath. 'I...I have a confession to make, and as a pastor of this church, I am obligated to come humbly in your presence. These past few days had taught me the importance of humility and servitude. See, I was a proud man who demanded respect and reverence. The death...the passing of my father taught me that I was really alone, fighting my own pride and self-absorbed thinking. Little did I know that I was really fighting against myself. I thought that wealth was the solution. I found that having more was my way of coping from things I could not control.

See, my mother taught me that it's not what you do, not who you do it to, but it is what we have done to make our brothers and sisters in Christ better. No one cares what we have, when we'll die, or about the wealth we earned. At the end, nothing matters more than the relationships we build. My mother taught me that, and I have forgotten. For that, I am truly shameful to preach the good news. These last few days taught me that the ones you loved can slip past this life without you knowing until you stand beside their lifeless body.

See, back there? There's a man sitting over there, and he's givin' it all for our freedom. He's sacrificed his life. He's my brother, and I am deeply proud of him. We have been honored by the presence of a silent hero. He knows what it is like to lose a close relative, to lose those whom you loved, and he taught me that that's what makes it a sweeter life. The bitterness of death gives us a taste of life when we live for those whom we cherish, including strangers.

So, my message to you is this...even if you forget what I just have said. I pray that you will take the time and make the effort to rebuild that crumbling relationship because at the end, when the world has ceased to turn, we can embrace those who touched us in the presence of God Almighty."

Marlon sat still and soaked in his brother's every word. As the sermon ended and as the people stood up to sing a hymn song, he quietly walked out. As he exited, he noticed his brother standing at the side of the podium, singing. Charles glanced over to him. Marlon smiled back, and Charles grinned and nodded. *"Behold, old things has passed. What once died has risen, and now, all things are new."* Marlon thought.

The following day, Marlon arrived at the street where he once frequented. He parked his truck at the opposite side of the gutter. Then he sat back, staring intently at the front door of an old white house. The house appeared vacated; it's overgrown, front-lawn was crowded with weeds and dirt patches, the cracks on the pavement were invaded by dandelions, and the wooden patio has withered from neglect, the plants wilted over the water stained planter nestled on the footsteps. *"Well, at least there's grass,"* he thought.

He left the engine running as he stared with glee at the front door, cherishing past memories. Then a song came on the radio. He hesitated for a moment, the words roused his emotions. He raised the volume, "Broken" by Lifehouse blared on the stereo. Then tears rolled down his face up until the song ended. It was just the right song he needed to hear to push him over the threshold.

He took his father's suitcase sitting on the passenger seat, stepped out of the vehicle, and carefully navigated his way to the front door. He hesitated for a moment, he peeked through dusted glass and knocked on the wooden door.

That noon, Cheryl was preparing lunch at her kitchen. Her daughter was sitting in the living room watching cartoons. She was easily mused, absorbing the characters and reciprocating with broken words at the small flickering screen. She didn't notice him standing at the porch, knocking repeatedly at the door. Cheryl wasn't expecting any guests to visit that dreary Sunday afternoon, but she kept the door cracked open to ventilate the musty air. The loud volume drowned out the footsteps and the door knocks. There was no doorbell, so Marlon kept knocking patiently as he looked on smiling. After several times, Cheryl finally heard the knocking and noticed a man's silhouette behind the door; his face was hidden behind the grimy stained-glass. She approached the door, as she called out to her daughter who was completely immersed with the television.

"Ensleigh! You're too close to the TV. Please sit on the sofa. You're too close to the TV, sweetheart."

She tuned the volume and walked toward the door. When she opened the door, her eyes widened as she gasped, utterly surprised to see him. "Mommy, is someone at the door?" Ensleigh asked with a gentle voice and innocent smile.

'Hi." Marlon smiled.

"Marlon!" she replied, still astonished to see her estranged husband.

"I wanted to…" He paused. "I want to come home."

Cheryl opened the screen door, her face beaming with excitement. Then she stepped outside the door and embraced him. "You are home," she whispered.

Marlon sighed, cracking a smile. "I want to come home and finish what I started." Tears rolled down his face. "This is my final stop."

Cheryl sobbed quietly and wiped the tears from her eyes as Ensleigh tugged on her skirt.

"Mommy, are you okay?"

"Daddy's home sweetheart. Daddy made it back."

Marlon saw the little girl and took her in his arms, and the three embraced.

Ensleigh was dumbfounded, her adorable bug-eyed expression made Marlon laugh. As she stared on her father's eyes, Marlon gently caressed her chin and softly kissed her on the lips. Then she grinned, and caressed his jaw with her petite hands, her effervescent disposition emanated through.

"Daddy,' Ensleigh innocently called out. 'Where you been?"

Marlon cried. "Daddy's been gone, sweetheart. Daddy got lost in the dark." Ensleigh smiled and stretched her bony arms around him. "Welcome home, Daddy!"

The three embraced. Marlon took his wife's hand and gently kissed her on the lips. Neither he nor his wife refrained each other. He looked at her and smiled. "I am home. I am home," he whispered.

Chapter Nineteen

Several months had passed since he stood by the doorway. An old man who lived down the street was walking his Jack Russell terrier on the sidewalk on a brisk Saturday morning. As he came by front paver, he stopped, and looked up at Marlon pounding nails on far side of the roof.

"The house looks great!" he yelled as he held fast on his dog's leash.

Marlon paused and nodded. "Thank you," he bellowed. He glanced around the rooftop, and wiped his forehead with his sleeve. "It's getting there. A few shingles here and there, and she'll be as good as new…after the new paint, of course."

The man resumed his route then stopped when he reached the mailbox. "Oh, by the way, how's the baby coming along?"

"He's getting bigger."

"Do you know when she'll be due?"

"A couple weeks or so."

"Got a name?"

Marlon smiled. "Eli. His name is Eli."

"Boy, that's quite a name."

"It is."

"Carries a lot of promise. Sounds powerful."

"It does, doesn't it?"

"Well, I better let you get back to work. Okay, good talk." The man waived and went on his way.

"Marlon!" his wife called out from the back porch with her hands resting on her back hips. She was eight months pregnant and her face was effervescent.

"Yeah!"

"There's a message for you."

"Who was it?"

"It's Charles. He said they'll be here in an hour."

"Okay, I should be done here soon."

"Okay, I'll let him know. Please, be careful up there."

Marlon chuckled. "Babe, this is nothing. As a matter of fact, this helps me relieve my stress."

"Well, you won't be too stressed if you fall. Actually, you're stressing me out...being up there." She smiled.

"It's so peaceful up here. Some married guys actually love this."

"That's why they get yelled at."

"What? I didn't get that." He smiled.

"Yea, that's funny." She replied sarcastically.

"I'll be right down."

"Alright, I got ya."

That afternoon, Charles, Darcy, and their two children arrived at the house. The two brothers embraced, and the family sat outside under the shady willow tree at the backyard. After a brief snack, as the children played on the backyard, Charles looked intently at Marlon.

"How are you doing?" Charles bluntly asked.

"Couldn't be better, Charles."

"Good, it's good to see you and your family coming along."

"It's been a good year, a bright, promising year."

"Do you miss it?"

Marlon lowered his head and paused briefly and made a deep sigh. "A bit. I miss the men, but I don't miss the action."

"What'd you mean by that?"

"Well, there's a part of me that wants this. That life in the past, is the past. But my men, I often wonder about them. How they're doing, their personal lives and their families. It makes me wonder, and that's what I missed."

Charles took a sip of his iced tea. "I'm pretty sure they're doing alright."

Marlon nodded. "I hope so. I did everything I could to protect those men. I trained them and taught them everything I knew, how to fight, how to kill, how to finish."

"That's a good thing."

"I never taught them how to heal. I wish I had." He scoffed. "But I was sick myself." He pointed at the rooftop. "That keeps me grounded.' he gently squeezed his wife's hand. 'This…keeps me sane and even-keeled. And God, has healed my brokenness.' He paused, and then his eyes narrowed. 'Wanna know something? This may sound strange, but when I was there, when I was in front of the enemy's crosshairs, when all hell was coming for me, I felt this invisible protection around me, like…it felt so strong, so real…like a veil grazing every follicle on my skin. I felt the presence of God around me that fear was peeled away. I was able to think clearly without any doubt."

Charles smiled. "Amazin'! That's really great to hear, and only God can do that. I get bumps just hearing that." He paused and noticed his brother's deep contemplation and decided to change the subject. "You still doing your meetings?" he asked.

Marlon Smiled. "Every day I head off to volunteer an hour or two… sometimes more talking to vets at the old feed store…Helps me heal just talking about it, hearing and crying with them. It's a godsend."

Charles nodded. "And…how's business?"

Marlon perked up. "Couldn't be better, Charles. I've been terribly booked doing construction work. As a matter of fact, I'm searching for a few good men to help me with few more construction projects. It's been a tremendous blessing. What Pops taught us came in handy. No pun intended." He smiled.

"Have you looked or interviewed candidates?"

"I was actually going to ask you, if you know people you could recommend."

"I'm not from this place, you know that. How could I recommend someone I don't know?"

"Well, let your congregation know. If they're interested, they'll move."

"You're going to need a couple more trucks."

Marlon chuckled. "Right, that's another thing."

"Lot people love your work, baby," his wife said.

"I hope so.' Charles chuckled. 'How could you go wrong with *Special Forces construction*?"

Marlon smirked. "Well, hey, so long as they love the work being done."

Charles nodded in agreement. "Mom's really proud of you. Pops, I'm fairly certain, is looking down proudly."

Marlon raises his glass of lemonade. "Here's to Pops."

"Here's to you and your family…and Pops!" Charles yelled.

They raised their glasses together. "I'm glad you made it here, Charles. If you ever need someone to build a new beautiful house for you here in Georgia, you give me call."

"You'd be the first to know, little brother. But I ain't moving here." He smiled. Then Charles leaned closer. "So, tell me about this man you met on the train."

Marlon smiled. "There's nothing like it, but it was better than anything I could have imagine." He leaned closer and whispered. "It was…a glimpse of heaven."